PETAL PLUCKER

Funny, charming, and utterly captivating! I devoured this sparkling read.

— ANNIKA MARTIN, NEW YORK TIMES BESTSELLING AUTHOR

Petal Plucker was funny, entertaining, fresh and fan-yourself-worthy . . . Their enemies-to-lovers romance is both charming, tender and steamy, and you'll love both of these characters (and their families!) and their sigh-worthy happily ever after.

— MARY DUBÉ, CONTEMPORARILY EVER AFTER

Morland has created a masterpiece of a romance . . . one of my favorite [books] of the year.

— CRISTIINA READS

Humorous, raunchy, and refreshing, Petal Plucker has rightfully earned its way, in my opinion, as one of the best romantic comedy [books] this year.

— CAROL, TIL THE LAST PAGE

My One and Only

This book was gripping, well written & the chemistry between the characters sizzled throughout this wonderful read.

— AMAZON REVIEW

All I Want Is You

Another heartfelt, steamy, terrific story. This is an author who really knows how to create a story that catches a reader's attention and characters that capture her heart.

— BOOKADDICT

Taking a Chance on Love

Thea and Anthony are in for a surprise when it comes to the language of the heart . . . I am in awe.

— HOPELESS ROMANTIC BLOG

Then Came You

This story really pulled all my heartstrings. This was truly a beautiful story and makes you believe there really is true love out there.

— MEME CHANELL BOOK CORNER

ALSO BY IRIS MORLAND

ROMANTIC COMEDIES

He Loves Me, He Loves Me Not

Petal Plucker

War of the roses

LOVE EVERLASTING

including

THE YOUNGERS

Then Came You

Taking a Chance on Love

All I Want Is You

My One and Only

THE THORNTONS

The Nearness of You

The Very Thought of You

If I Can't Have You

Dream a Little Dream of Me

ALL I WANT IS YOU

THE YOUNGERS

IRIS MORLAND

BLUE VIOLET PRESS LLC

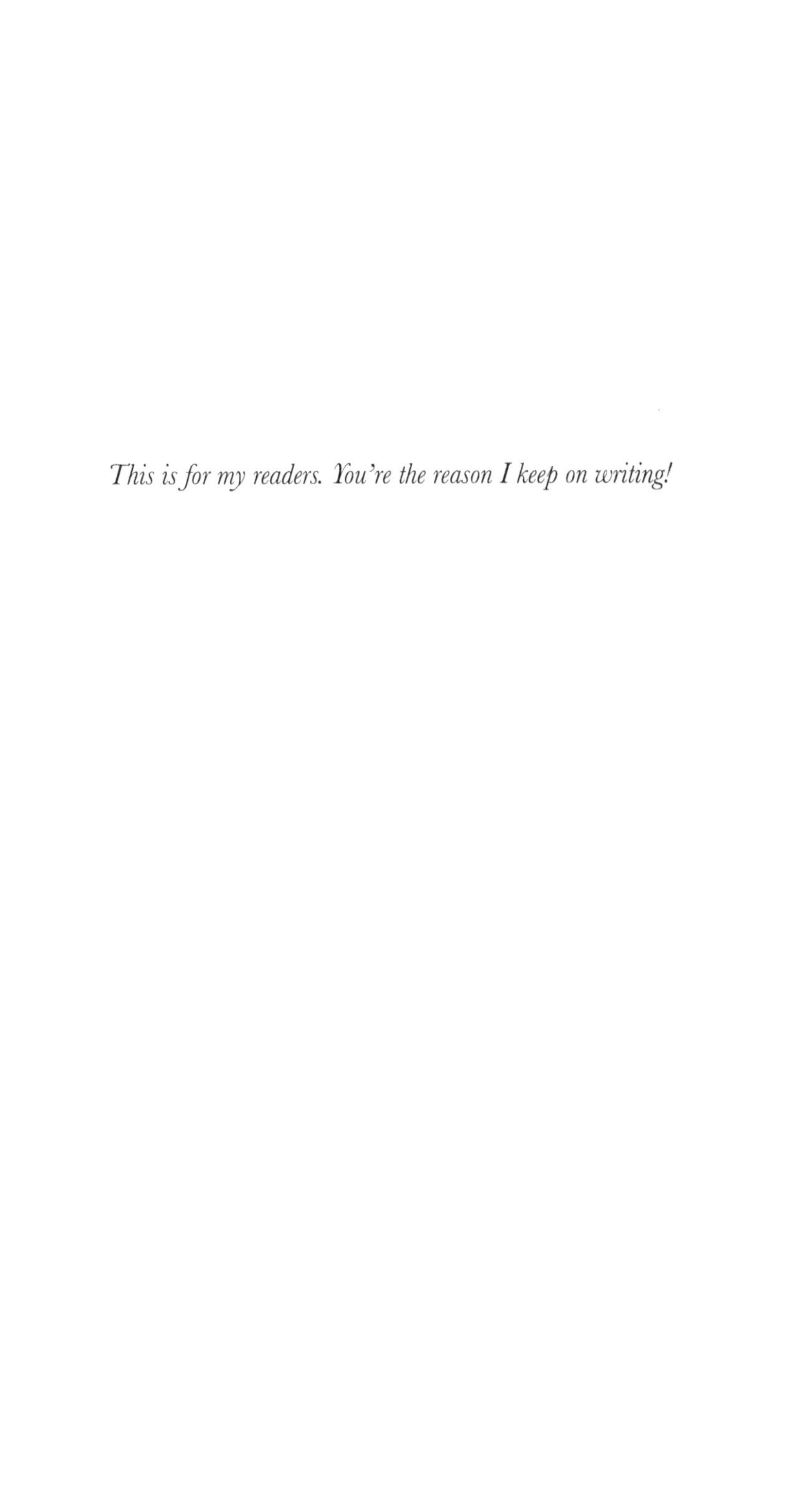

This is for my readers. You're the reason I keep on writing!

ALL I WANT IS YOU

Sighing deeply, her feet aching from standing all afternoon and evening, Emily Lassiter glanced at the clock on the wall of The Dine in Five and wanted to sigh all over again. She still had two hours left on her shift.

Normally her waitressing shifts went by quickly, but tonight there was a dearth of customers, which meant there was only so much work to do. Her boss, Lawrence, had already sent two other waitresses home. Emily was just glad that she got to work tonight—she needed the money rather desperately.

"Your table wants more ketchup," said Lawrence as he passed her in the hallway. Middle-aged and married with three kids, Lawrence had been like a father figure to Emily ever since she'd gotten this job two years ago. When he looked at her pale face, he added, "You okay, kid?"

Emily forced herself to smile. "Fine. Ketchup, you said? I'll go get that."

Lawrence looked like he didn't believe her, but thankfully

his phone rang, effectively distracting him. Emily went to the kitchen and grabbed a full bottle of ketchup.

The table in question had four guys about Emily's age—four guys who'd been ogling her since the second she'd taken their orders. Emily was no stranger to male attention, something she both loved and hated for various reasons. Hated, because men tended to see only a pretty face and nothing else. Loved, because it had opened doors for her to become a model. Unfortunately, her few years of modeling had gone nowhere, and now here she was, waitressing and scraping together a living for herself and her younger brother, Josh.

"Here you go," she said, setting the ketchup on the table. "You guys need anything else?"

One guy with a buzzed head and cleft chin eyed her up and down. Emily restrained from crossing her arms over her chest when his gaze lingered on her breasts.

"You work here long?" the buzz-cut man asked. "I haven't seen you here before."

Emily barely stopped herself from rolling her eyes. "For a few years. You guys enjoy your meal."

Emily was tempted to tell Lawrence about this group, but she was tired of going to him when a male customer hit on her. Sometimes she blamed herself for the attention. Had she smiled too much? Given some kind of hint that she was interested? She always made certain to be polite and friendly, nothing more, but a niggle of doubt always bloomed inside her.

Her customers now occupied with eating, she stepped outside into the cool night air for her break. Although it was July in Portland, the nights edged toward chilly sometimes.

Emily wished she'd put on her sweater before stepping outside.

But the cold disappeared from her mind as she began to calculate on her phone how much she'd already made tonight, adding it to the running total for the week. Tonight being so slow meant she'd make a lot less in tips, and when she saw the final pathetic number on her phone's calculator, she wanted to cry. She was already on thin ice with her landlord as it was. The last three months, she'd paid the rent late, and he'd warned her that if she did it a fourth time, he'd evict her and Josh.

That was the last thing she or Josh needed. Her younger brother, who had just turned sixteen, was both the love of her life and the bane of her existence. After their mother had died nine years ago, their father having passed away when Josh was a baby, Emily had become more of a mother to her brother than a sister. Josh had been a sweet, shy boy, interested in building trains and not much else. Within the last year, he'd not only shot up in height, but he'd gotten involved with a group of boys that had brought him nothing but trouble.

Now her sweet baby brother was an angry teenager who skipped school, smoked, drank, and refused to do anything Emily told him to do. Just that morning, she'd gotten a call from Josh's high school, telling her that he was practically failing everything except physical education. If he didn't do something to improve his grades, he'd have to redo eleventh grade.

Emily rubbed her temples. She couldn't even help her brother with his grades, considering that she hadn't graduated from high school, either. She could barely even read, although she'd done her best to keep that a secret from everyone, including Josh.

She could always do those photos for Landon, her ex-boyfriend. Landon had promised her a hefty sum if she'd do nude photos for him. Emily had always told him no, not because she thought posing nude was wrong per se, but because that wasn't the type of modeling she wanted to do. She preferred modeling clothes, not her body. It was a different set of skills, anyway, the ability to show off a dress or a top, versus showing off everything that God had given her.

But right then, she was tempted to take Landon's offer. What did it matter, anyway? She needed the money, Landon *had* the money, and it'd be a quick way to get it.

And yet, she hesitated. Maybe that made her stupid, but right then, she'd prefer to be stupid than go against her own principles. Smiling bitterly, she realized that a person could only keep to their principles for so long until they were hungry enough not to care.

Emily took another deep breath, then another, trying to center herself. She couldn't break down right now. She needed to keep smiling so she'd get good tips. And if she was good at anything, it was making people feel at ease with her pretty smile and melodic voice.

Returning inside the diner, she cleared plates and brought checks to the group of four guys. Emily hoped that the buzz-cut man would give up on getting her number, but when she came back with their receipts to sign, he said, "You got a boyfriend? Because if you don't, you should give me your number."

She could smell alcohol on his breath as he leaned toward

her. She took a step back as she shook her head. "I'm taken," she lied. "Sorry about that."

She'd found that men tended to leave her alone if she said she was claimed, like she was an object that someone had already called dibs on. It rankled, but it was better than men continuing to hit on her.

Buzz-cut man, though, wasn't going to be put off that easily. "I don't see a ring," he said. His grin turned to a leer. "Come on, sweetie. I saw how you looked at me. Don't play dumb with me."

"I'm taken," she said more firmly. "You guys have a good night." She said the words in her coldest tone, and anyone with an ounce of brain cells could tell she was serious.

The buzz-cut man scowled. "Bitch," he muttered. "You're not that pretty anyway."

Emily had heard every insult under the sun. She simply ignored the man, focusing on the new table of customers who were, thankfully, all women.

Later, Emily collected the receipts from the guys' table, and when she opened them to check for tips, she realized that all four had left her zero tips. The buzz-cut man's receipt read, *No tips for bitches*, on the line for the tip amount. It took her a long moment to read what the man had written, and she was glad nobody was watching her try to read it. That only made things worse.

When Emily finally deciphered what it said, she turned scarlet with anger. She swallowed against sudden tears. It was stupid, letting this get to her. When Lawrence came out of the kitchen, she forced back the tears. She wouldn't let guys like that ruin her night.

The rest of the night went smoothly, and although Emily

ended the night with less tips than usual, it wasn't as terrible as she'd been expecting. Lawrence handed her the stack of cash after going through the receipts.

"Here," he said, handing her an extra twenty-dollar bill. "For those assholes who didn't tip you."

"Oh, you don't have to—"

"No, but I'm going to. You know you can always tell me when guys harass you."

His probing look made her glance away; she shrugged. "If I came to you every time, you wouldn't do anything else."

"Well, that's what I'm here for." He patted her shoulder awkwardly.

Emily was on the bus home when her phone rang. Considering how late it was and that she didn't recognize the number, she let it go to voicemail. The same number called her a second time, though, and she picked up with an annoyed, "Hello?"

"Is this Emily Lassiter?"

Emily didn't recognize the voice on the other end. Was it a bill collector? Her blood froze. Or was it somebody from her apartment, telling her she was getting kicked out? She stuttered out *yes* and waited for the bad news, never expecting what she'd actually hear.

"This is Officer Monroe at the Multnomah County Detention Center. Your brother has been arrested and is in our custody."

Emily was glad she was sitting down; otherwise she would've collapsed onto the floor of the bus from shock. *Arrested?* "Oh God, what did he do? Is he okay? Can I talk to him?"

"He's fine, ma'am." The officer cleared his throat, and

Emily heard voices in the background. "He was pulled over this afternoon after a friend of his was allegedly involved in a robbery. Your brother was the driver of the getaway vehicle."

"I want to talk to him. Is he there? Can I come see him?"

"I'm sorry, ma'am, no. He'll have a hearing that will include any charges filed against him within twenty-four hours. You'll be able to see him then." The man paused before adding, "I'd recommend finding an attorney immediately, if I were you."

Emily's heart sank into her toes. "I can't afford a lawyer," she whispered.

"Then your brother will be appointed one by the county. Let me have you talk to Harry here. He'll fill you in on everything you need to know about what'll happen going forward."

By the time Emily arrived home, she could only sit down on her threadbare couch and stare at the wall. The adrenaline that had been racing through her body had turned to ice in her veins. She'd heard the words *felony* and *tried as an adult* and *aiding and abetting* and all she'd wanted to do was talk to Josh, to hear his side of the story, to understand what had really happened.

Emily put her head in her hands, her shoulders shaking. She'd never felt so out of her depth, so terrified of something she had no knowledge of. She'd never even gotten so much as a speeding ticket, and here her baby brother was, arrested and facing serious charges.

Her head pounded. Exhaustion swamped her until she could barely find the energy to get up from the couch and go to her bedroom. Before she did, though, she went to Josh's room, staring at the empty bed—never made, of course—the desk covered in everything but schoolwork. Posters of bands that Emily had never heard of hung on the walls, while clothes were scattered over the floor. She sat down on his bed, and she smiled even as tears pricked her eyes when she saw the photo of herself and Josh on his nightstand.

Josh had been twelve in the photo, and Emily had still been modeling. She touched Josh's face in the photo, a sob breaking through. Where had her little brother gone? And what if she couldn't get him back?

She clutched the photo to her chest, lying down on Josh's bed, inhaling the teenage boy scent that permeated the sheets. She wished her mom were alive, although part of her was glad she wouldn't see her son like this. No, this would've broken their mom's heart; she'd had such big plans for both Emily and Josh.

Tears leaking from her eyes, Emily held the photo close until she fell into a restless slumber.

CHAPTER TWO

Phin Younger tapped his pen against the table as he waited for somebody from the DA's office to show up for this court case. Phin's client, a sixteen-year-old who'd been the driver of a getaway car for his friend who'd committed a robbery—slumped in his chair despite Phin's admonition that he should sit up.

Josh Lassiter was tall and bulky for his age and looked much older than sixteen. He had a sulky turn to his mouth that Phin had recognized the second he'd shaken the kid's hand and introduced himself as his court-appointed lawyer. Josh had sneered and told him in no uncertain terms that he was wasting his time.

Phin often felt like he was wasting his time—or rather, like he was fighting a losing battle with these cases. As a court-appointed lawyer who worked in the county's public defender's office, Phin got the cases of people who couldn't afford a fancy lawyer. Phin was his client's only chance at either getting out of prison or at least getting less time. But with more and more cases piling onto his desk, Phin could only help so many people. And there were always too many people needing help.

The courtroom door opened and, turning, Phin watched a harried woman hurry down the aisle toward them. Her dark hair was falling out of a bun, and her blouse was lopsided; she'd most likely missed a button in her haste.

"Mr. Younger?" the woman said as she approached Phin.

Josh muttered something, and it took Phin only a moment to put two and two together. This must be Josh's sister, his legal guardian. "Yes," said Phin as he stood and shook the woman's hand. "Nice to meet you."

"I'm Emily Lassiter." She looked over Phin's shoulder, her gaze worried as she tried to catch Josh's eye. Her brother was studiously not looking at her; her shoulders slumped. "Thank you for your help," she said sincerely.

Despite her rumpled appearance, Emily Lassiter was absolutely gorgeous. Ridiculously, absurdly, unbelievably gorgeous. There were too many adverbs to describe her beauty, if he were honest. Phin stared down at her, suddenly struggling to find the words to reply to her. Seeing her up close was rather like getting hit by a train.

There was no other way to describe it. Even with her hair a mess and her blouse lopsided, she had the widest, prettiest green eyes he'd ever seen. With her heart-shaped face, high cheekbones, and milky skin, she could've graced the pages of some magazine. Even her nose was pretty: tilted slightly upward, it was as delicate as the rest of her.

As someone who worked with the public, Phin had learned how to talk to people, despite it not being his greatest strength. He'd learned that men respected frankness with a touch of arrogance, while women preferred a kinder approach

—less frank, more conciliatory. Phin had worked with people from all walks of life: from high-powered executives to criminals who'd never known an ounce of kindness in their entire lives.

He'd worked with nice people, annoying people, stupid people, mean people. He'd learned how to use language to make people do what he wanted, something he'd struggled to do as a child who was too cripplingly shy and awkward to string coherent sentences together.

This ability he'd supposedly perfected apparently didn't stretch to women he found attractive. And Jesus Christ, Emily Lassiter looked like she'd stepped out of a painting into this dingy courtroom.

Swallowing, his mind racing, Phin shuffled some papers on his desk before finally saying bluntly, "You should sit down before the judge gets annoyed."

The judge was drinking coffee as he waited for some bit of paperwork to read over, but Emily blushed all the same and sat down without another word. Phin wanted to kick himself. When he saw Josh smirking at him, Phin wanted to tell the boy to mind his own damn business.

"What's taking so long?" said Josh as they waited. "Why did I have to get up this fucking early for no reason?"

"Most of what's going to happen going forward is going to be you waiting," said Phin quietly.

Finally, the hearing began.

"Since you are accused of having assisted in the crime of robbery in the second degree, Mr. Lassiter," the judge said, "you'll be charged with aiding and abetting, which falls under the Ballot 11 measure and is a class B felony. This also means that, since you are above the age of fifteen, you could be tried as an adult and could face up to five years and ten months in prison as a result."

Phin heard Emily inhale sharply. He wished he'd had time to prepare her, but between Josh and his ten other clients, he hadn't gotten a chance to contact her.

"Considering that Mr. Lassiter has been suspended from school four times now and has run away from home twice, I'm setting the bail at one hundred thousand dollars, ten percent of which must be posted for Mr. Lassiter to be released," said the judge. "That being said, the defendant will stay in juvenile detention for now, instead of being transferred to prison, assuming good behavior."

Phin sighed inwardly. He'd hoped the judge would be lenient in terms of the bail, but he'd known that nothing less than fifty thousand dollars would have been allowable based on the charges. At least Josh wouldn't be moved to an adult prison—that was one thing to celebrate.

When the hearing was over, Phin said to Josh, "I'll talk to you soon, all right? Most likely later this week."

Josh shrugged, although Phin knew the kid was terrified. His face was ghostly pale, and as the guard led him out of the courtroom, Josh stumbled over his feet. Phin's heart pinched at the sight. The kid had made a stupid mistake with grave consequences.

Most people didn't know that in Oregon, certain crimes came with mandatory sentences, and being under the age of eighteen didn't exempt you, either. Phin disagreed with the law, especially in terms of juveniles, but all he could do was work within the system and help his young clients as much as humanly possible.

Gathering his briefcase and papers, Phin looked up to see Emily in front of him.

"Could Josh really go to prison for six years?" she asked, her green eyes wide with fear. She looked wan, dark circles under her pretty eyes. "For just driving away?"

"Unfortunately, yes." Phin winced. "I apologize, but I have another hearing to get to right now. Please call my office and set up an appointment for later this week so we can discuss further. I can't talk specifics now, but I have reason to hope that we can get the judge to agree to a plea deal so this doesn't go to trial." He reached inside his suit jacket and handed Emily his card.

Her shoulders slumped. "Thank you. Are you saying Josh might not go to jail?"

"It's hard to say at this point. Like I said, I can discuss further with you at our appointment." Realizing he sounded brusque, he softened his tone. "I've seen worse cases, Ms. Lassiter. Don't give up hope."

Her chin wobbled. "I'm trying, but I feel like my hope is getting crushed no matter what I do."

"Don't give up hope," he repeated. Seeing her wet eyes and quivering lower lip, Phin wished he could do something for her. Give her a hug, at least, although that would be inappropriate. Tapping the card in her hand, he said, "Call my office. I'll see you soon."

Despite two more hearings that day, Phin couldn't stop thinking about Emily Lassiter. He told himself it was just because she was pretty, he was a heterosexual male, and he was as shallow as any man. He remembered the curve of her lip, the freckles on her cheeks, the sweep of her dark lashes.

She'd had a beauty mark near her mouth that he'd wanted to taste.

I need to get ahold of myself. She's not for me.

Despite Phin's belief that love and all of the emotions related to that feeling were both messy and pointless, that didn't mean he didn't want sex, either. It had been a while, admittedly. Maybe he just needed to get laid, with all of this thinking about his client's gorgeous sister.

Blowing out a breath, he was about to leave the courthouse to return to the office when he ran into the last person he wanted to see: Sterling McIntosh, fellow lawyer, former law school classmate, and a smarmy son of a bitch who Phin loathed. Luckily, the feeling was mutual.

Phin had heard that Sterling had recently gotten a job at the county district attorney's office. It still surprised him that anyone would hire Sterling, considering his less-than-sterling reputation, but it helped that his father was golf buddies with the governor.

"Long time no see, Younger," said Sterling. "How's it going?"

"As you see me," said Phin dryly. "I'm going back to the office."

"The hero of the poor and downtrodden fights on," mocked Sterling. "How do you manage to pay your bills? I'm curious."

"Just like anyone else: I actually *work.*"

Sterling's smile twisted. They both knew that Sterling preferred the title of lawyer more than the actual work.

"You still think you're hot shit, don't you? When we both know you aren't getting paid more than some checkout boy at the local grocery store." Sterling stepped closer to him.

Although Sterling was about half a head shorter than Phin, he was muscular and probably weighed as much as him. Not that Phin had ever imagined decking the guy in the face.

Sterling said in a low voice, "Don't think I've forgotten what you did to me. You almost got me kicked out of law school over some stupid rule—"

"Criminal offense, actually."

"And you have the gall to act like you're better than me?" Sterling's eyes flashed. "This is the last thing I'll say to you: you better watch yourself. Because the second you step out of line? I'll know about it, and you'll regret it."

Sterling pushed past Phin, Phin wishing he'd given into his baser instincts and punched the guy already. So Sterling was still pissed about what had happened years ago? Fine. Sterling was like a rooster in the henhouse: a lot of crowing until he came up against a bigger, smarter rooster.

Phin never stepped out of line, anyway. He did everything by the book—his personal life included. But as he thought of how orderly and by the rules his life was, Emily's face flashed in his mind. It reminded him that even a straitlaced lawyer like himself could be tempted to break the rules if given enough incentive.

CHAPTER THREE

Emily tried to calm her racing heart as she waited to see Josh's lawyer later that week. When Mr. Younger had told her that Josh could go to prison for close to six years, she'd wanted to throw up. He wasn't even eighteen yet! And he hadn't even been the one to rob that store. How could that be fair or just?

"Ms. Lassiter?" Mr. Younger entered the tiny waiting room at the public defender's office. "Come on back."

Emily followed him, once again admiring how young and handsome he was. When she'd first seen him in the courtroom, she'd almost demanded to know how old he was because he seemed too young to know what he was doing. She'd been afraid he wasn't really a lawyer but instead some intern practicing on her poor brother. But, no, according to everything she'd found online, Phineas Younger, J.D., was as much a lawyer as she was a broke waitress and former model. He'd graduated at the top of his class from the University of Oregon, and he'd been working as a public defender since he'd passed the bar.

As they entered his office, the sunlight streaming through the only window, Phin's hair gleamed. Emily had never seen a shade like that: it was strawberry blond, but depending on the light, it either looked pure red or pure blond. Right then, the sunlight made the auburn strands sparkle. It was ridiculous, really.

Emily had to force her thoughts away from admiring her brother's lawyer's hair like a total idiot. *Stop gawking at the lawyer, Em.*

"Right. Have a seat." Phin sat down in front of his desk, which was immaculate in its organization, color-coded files placed in various bins and organizers. Pens were lined up next to his left hand, while a calendar with neat handwriting took up much of the room on the desk. Emily looked around, her gaze landing on the bookshelf that took up the entire southern wall.

Trying to make out the titles and knowing it was hopeless, she suddenly felt intimidated. Of course she knew Phin was smart: he was a lawyer, for God's sake. But the books were like a flashing signal that screamed at her that she was out of her depth.

"Your brother, to put it mildly, is in a difficult spot," said Phin as he opened a file, not wasting any time. He scanned a document, his lips thinning as he read through it.

"As I mentioned at the hearing, despite Josh's age, he would be tried as an adult since second-degree robbery has a mandatory sentence if convicted, and Josh knew that his friend planned to rob the store, too. The fact that Josh and his companion were pulled over by the police and the stolen merchandise was found in the trunk, along with the more serious charge of Mr. Berkley threatening violence toward the sales clerk during the robbery, doesn't help, either."

When Emily had spoken with Josh yesterday at the detention center, Josh had insisted that it had all been his best friend Reggie's idea. This hadn't surprised Emily, considering that Reggie seemed to be the instigator of Josh's skipping school and running away. Emily had tried to get Josh to stop hanging out with Reggie, but short of locking Josh in his room, she couldn't watch over her brother constantly and work to pay their bills.

After meeting with Josh yesterday at the detention center, Emily had finally heard the entire story behind the robbery. Josh hadn't wanted to talk about it, but Emily had badgered him until he'd given in.

According to Josh, during an afternoon when the two boys skipped school, Reggie came up with the plan of stealing from a local department store. "All you have to do is take shit to the dressing room, because there aren't any cameras there," he'd told Josh.

When Reggie had told Josh that they could steal small, expensive items like perfume and sell them for extra cash, Josh had finally agreed. It had seemed like a straightforward plan. Reggie had insisted that his cousin stole from places all the time and that was how he got most of his money.

After some discussion, Reggie decided he would be the one stealing; Josh would drive Reggie's cousin's car when Reggie came out of the store. It was a simple enough plan: steal bottles of cologne and perfume along with any other small items that Reggie could fit into his oversized jeans pockets. Easy in, easy out.

The plan seemed to go off without a hitch. Reggie stole

hundreds of dollars' worth of merchandise and walked out of the store without incident. Josh had noticed that Reggie seemed on edge as he'd gotten into the car, swearing at Josh when he hadn't driven off fast enough. That was when Josh had noticed the knife in Reggie's hand.

Reggie had denied threatening anyone, but deep inside, Josh had known otherwise. Reggie had insisted that they celebrate their victory. They hadn't gotten caught, had they?

But their victory had only lasted for so long. Josh had pushed aside the thought of the knife.

Josh was so excited at how much Reggie had stolen for them both that he didn't realize he was speeding. When a cop pulled him over for going twice the limit, Reggie almost bolted right then and there.

The boys weren't good enough actors to fool the police officer. At their edgy and nervous looks, he asked them to step out of the vehicle, and within moments, the officer found the stolen merchandise. He'd already gotten a call about a robbery, and he identified Reggie as the person at large. Within minutes, both Josh and Reggie were arrested.

Sitting in Phin's office, Emily wished she could go to the detention center and shake her brother until his teeth rattled. She'd wanted to do exactly that yesterday. How could he have been so stupid?

Emily rubbed her sweaty palms against her dress. "I still don't understand why Josh would be charged with robbery, too. He didn't steal anything—Reggie did."

"But he knew Reggie had planned to rob that store, and he helped him get away. That's more than enough in the eyes of the law," said Phin.

"So that's it?" She felt tears of despair prick her eyelids. "Josh will go to prison no matter what?"

Phin's voice was gentle as he said, "Most likely, but since he wasn't the one who committed the robbery itself, that gives us a little leeway. I believe a plea deal is in his best interest in this case. He can plead to a lesser charge so this doesn't go to trial, and then it also doesn't fall under a Ballot 11 measure. He'd be tried a juvenile, which is about rehabilitation, not punishment."

Emily listened as Phin spoke at length about plea deals, sentencing, and all kinds of legal jargon that went over Emily's head. By the time he was finished speaking, she felt like her brain was completely overloaded.

"It can't be that easy. Josh takes a plea deal, and that's it?"

Phin smiled grimly. "Well, we can try. The judge doesn't have to accept it."

At that thought, Emily felt a bubble of hysteria building inside her. The burden of everything weighed on her until she wanted to collapse under its weight. She wondered if this was what it felt like to drown—one minute you were breathing oxygen, the next, your throat closed as the water rushed in and filled your lungs.

The thought of Josh in prison shot straight to her heart. And their mom—she'd be devastated if she were alive. Emily had failed their mom as surely as she'd failed Josh.

To Emily's immense humiliation, tears filled her eyes until she started crying right in Phin's office. She couldn't stop crying even if she wanted to. It was like a dam had burst and the river had to run its course.

"I'm sorry," said Phin quietly as he placed a box of tissues in front of her. "I'll do the best I can for your brother. I promise you that."

Emily just cried harder. She grabbed a handful of tissues to wipe her face, but it was no use. She couldn't stop crying.

Finally, her sobs turned to hiccups, and then she was dabbing at her reddened eyes and blowing her nose as she tried to put herself to rights. She blushed scarlet when she looked up to see Phin watching her, his own expression one of secondhand embarrassment tinged with dismay.

Emily sniffled. "God, I'm sorry. I didn't come here just to cry in your office. I'm a mess." She grabbed more tissues, like they could ward off more tears. "I'm not usually a crier."

"You're not the first person to cry in my office, Ms. Lassiter, and I doubt you'll be the last."

She laughed a little. "I guess that's reassuring."

"At least you didn't throw a book at my head."

"Someone threw a book at you?" She stared at him, incredulous.

"She was… distraught. Luckily it was a paperback, and she had terrible aim."

"I'm not sure why someone would want to throw something at you. I'd rather throw something at my brother."

"Ms. Lassiter," said Phin, his expression turning serious. "I meant what I said. I know a court-appointed lawyer seems like the short end of the stick, and I won't lie and say that that's not often the case. There aren't enough of us to go around. But I don't do this job for the glory: I do it because I want to help people who need help the most. The people who are forgotten in the system."

He sounded so sincere, so passionate, that Emily's overburdened heart lifted a little at the words. When had she last been able to rely on someone else? Too long. Since her mother had died, really. Emily had taken care of herself and Josh without any help.

There had been a few boyfriends who'd come and gone, but they'd never been reliable. They'd buy Emily trinkets and tell her she was beautiful, but when they realized she had to focus on paying her bills and taking care of an annoying younger brother instead of paying attention to them, the boyfriends inevitably left her for greener pastures.

"Thank you for all of your help. And please, call me Emily."

Phin smiled. "You're welcome, Emily."

Hearing her name on his lips felt almost like a caress. They stared at each other, the moment lengthening, until Phin glanced at his computer screen and said, "I have another appointment, but let me walk you out."

Desire flashed in his eyes, but only for a second. She knew that flash almost as much as she knew her own reflection: it was how men always looked at her. But Emily was tired of men seeing her merely as a pretty face and body, with no brain or personality. Phin was hardly like any of her exes, but she knew men: they were all the same in the essentials.

Caught between feeling flattered and frustrated that even this man would only see her as a pretty face and nothing more, she saw Phin reach behind her to hand her her forgotten sweater.

"No, I'll get it," she blurted. She grabbed the sweater up before he could touch it, and she instantly regretted the action, like his touching her things disgusted her.

His face closed. The softness in his expression instantly

hardened. She wanted to apologize, but she felt so awkward that she was tongue-tied.

"If you have any questions, please don't hesitate to contact me," he said as they entered the waiting room, now brusque and formal. He glanced at his watch, like he was already dismissing her from his mind. "Have a nice afternoon, Ms. Lassiter."

So it was already back to Ms. Lassiter, not Emily. Emily almost called him back to apologize, but he'd already walked away. She stood there, uncertain, until the woman at the front desk asked her if she needed anything.

Feeling stupid, Emily muttered a noncommittal answer and told herself that getting entangled with any man—let alone her brother's lawyer—would be the height of idiocy. No matter how nicely he filled out a suit, or how his hair gleamed in the sunlight, or how kind he'd looked for an instant before she'd ruined the moment.

CHAPTER FOUR

Phin had lied about having another appointment because he'd needed to get Emily out of his office. She presented too much of a temptation to him, which bothered him immensely. He wasn't the type of guy who was easily tempted. He kept to himself, and it had worked for twenty-eight years of his life.

When he sat down heavily in his office chair, he stared at nothing for a long moment. Until a voice broke through his disordered thoughts.

"Who's the new client?" Katherine, Phin's coworker and only real friend within the office, sat down on the edge of his desk with a smile. Happily married with kids, Katherine was somehow convinced that everyone else needed the same things in life to be happy.

Phin, however, had so far resisted her best efforts to pair him up with one of her girlfriends.

"Sixteen-year-old brother arrested for aiding and abetting a robbery," he replied.

Katherine whistled. "Damn. That's serious. You gonna do a plea?"

"Most likely. I'm not sure we have any other option."

"And that was his mother…?"

Phin shook his head. "No, sister."

"Interesting."

Phin ignored Katherine for the time being. If she wanted to say something, she would. She always did.

When Phin had first joined the office, he'd been uninterested in going out to office happy hours and attending potlucks at people's homes on the weekends, which hadn't made him popular. Phin found mindless socializing to be annoying at best, painful at worst. It wasn't that he didn't care about his coworkers. They weren't friends, though. He preferred to keep it that way.

But the office was small—staff included Katherine, Dave, Jerry, their boss, Linda, and the front desk woman, Tammy, along with Phin—and Phin had entered into an already tight-knit group when he'd been hired. His aloofness hadn't made him popular, and soon, Dave and Tammy, the most extroverted and prone to planning potlucks, had stopped inviting him to shindigs entirely.

Katherine had been the only one to draw him out of his shell. Where Dave and Tammy had been offended by Phin's disinterest in their invitations, Katherine had realized that Phin simply wasn't comfortable in social situations that weren't strictly business. Phin had never said as much to Katherine, but she was perceptive.

Too perceptive, given the speculative gleam in her eye right now.

"I got a glimpse of her. She's gorgeous. Like, ridiculously beautiful."

"So why don't you date her?" drawled Phin.

Katherine grinned. "My husband probably wouldn't love that arrangement. No, I'm just saying that I saw that look on your face. I've never seen that on your face, ever."

"How would you know? Have you seen my face every moment in the last twenty-odd years?"

She rolled her eyes. "If you're interested in this woman—"

"I'm not."

"Then you should ask her out."

"Katherine, she's a *client.*"

"She won't be for long. Besides, you can date clients. It's not against the rules."

"It's still a bad idea."

"Fine, wait until everything is done with her brother. Then ask her out. What do you have to lose?"

Phin knew very well that a woman as beautiful as Emily would have no interest in some socially awkward lawyer like him. Besides, when he'd tried to hand her her sweater, she'd acted like he had the plague. That wasn't a woman who would say yes to going out for a drink.

"I'm not asking Emily out because she's a client," he said again, "and because I'm not interested in her. I'm too busy for dating anyway. Did you need something else?"

Katherine shrugged and got off his desk. "No, but just a reminder that even somebody like you can't live your entire life without any companionship. Humans are social animals. You aren't an island, Phin. Nobody is."

After work, Phin considered Katherine's words as he sat outside on his tiny apartment deck and watched the sunset.

Although his apartment was small, he'd chosen this place for the view of downtown Portland and the Willamette River curling lazily around it. He'd grown up in Washington State, but he'd moved to Oregon for college over a decade ago. Portland had quickly become home, its quirkiness and vast array of people in contrast to small-town living in tiny Fair Haven, Washington.

Despite living in a large city now, Phin had managed to be an island for his entire life. The only people he really cared about were his siblings—Trent, Thea, Ash and Lucy—and even then, sometimes he felt like he was obligated to care for them because he shared DNA with them. He'd envied only children sometimes. They didn't have to worry about siblings constantly wanting to know about your business.

He grimaced at how cold that sounded. His brothers would tell him he was an arrogant piece of shit for thinking that, and they'd be right. Even though Phin struggled to understand Trent's need for absolution with their now-deceased father, or Ash's love of sleeping with any woman who so much looked at him sideways until he'd met his fiancée, Violet, Phin still loved his brothers and his sisters regardless.

Despite Phin's insistence to Katherine that he preferred to be a loner, there was a niggling feeling in the back of his mind that wouldn't let up. If he was entirely honest with himself, he'd felt lonely lately. He came home from work to a silent apartment, the weight of the day's work on his shoulders, and he almost wished he could talk to somebody about it. And, yes, maybe enjoy the embrace of a woman along with the talking.

Women, though? They wanted more than Phin could give.

They wanted security, compliments, attention. They wanted sweet words, grand gestures. They wanted not just your time, but your heart cut out of your chest for them to use as they saw fit.

Phin smiled wryly. His sisters would slap him upside the head for the thought. What women really wanted, though, was the one word that made him shudder: commitment.

Phin didn't have time for commitment. He hardly had time to buy groceries, let alone dedicate time to another person. He found fulfillment in helping other people who would never demand more than he could give.

As a child, Phin had watched his parents fall apart. Beatrice Younger had suffered from an undiagnosed mental illness. She'd only deteriorated further due to Edward Younger's propensity for hitting her when he was at his angriest and drunkest.

Phin had seen how Beatrice hadn't been able to get the help she'd needed from the system, and she'd killed herself in the end. Beatrice had died when Phin was ten. He'd decided at her funeral that he'd do his utmost to help people like her when he was older. Maybe he could make a difference. Maybe he could be that one person that kept someone from getting lost in the maze that was the system.

A memory resurfaced. When Phin had been six years old, he'd been home from school, sick with a cold. Beatrice had stayed with him, playing games with him to pass the time until they could get to the pediatrician later that afternoon. This had been before things had gotten really bad, when Beatrice hadn't spent most of her time in her room crying, or too high on pain pills to notice what was going on around her.

"Phin, did I tell you that your teacher called me?" she said as she placed letter blocks on the Scrabble board. "She says you should skip a grade."

Phin studied his own letters, barely hearing his mother. Despite being in first grade, Phin read at a fifth-grade level already. He sped through assignments with ease, and as a result, he tended to get in trouble because he was bored.

"I was thinking about it, and I think you should," continued Beatrice. She smiled as he formed the word *frigid* on the board. "What do you say, Phinny?"

Phin looked up. "What grade would I go to?"

"Second grade, although Mrs. Keller said that you'd do some more testing to make sure." Beatrice ruffled his hair. "My son the prodigy. I'm so proud of you. You'll do something great with that big brain of yours, I know it."

Phin swelled at the praise. While Trent and Ash were popular and athletic, Thea was artistic, and Lucy was simply adorable, Phin had always felt like he was the odd one out. He was too young to know what that feeling really meant, but he thought it was because he could read better than Ash already or because Thea liked to ask him to do her homework, before Beatrice had caught her and grounded her for it.

Phin had ended up skipping a grade, finishing high school at sixteen and graduating with his law degree by the time he was twenty-three. Because he'd been so advanced for his age, he'd struggled to make friends, especially as a teenager. By the time he'd gotten his law degree, he'd resigned himself to being alone.

Phin's reverie was interrupted when he heard something being shoved through his mail slot. Getting up, surprised that the mail was this late, he sorted through mostly junk until he came upon the last piece of mail. Phin smiled as he opened the thick vellum envelope, his name and address written in looping calligraphy.

You are cordially invited to attend the wedding of Ash Younger and Violet Fielding. The date and time followed. Didn't these fancy invitations always have the couple's full names?

Phin couldn't help but laugh a little when he realized that Ash had avoided including his entire given name on the invite. All of the Youngers had ridiculous names that they'd all shortened to more acceptable nicknames. Ash's full name was Ashley, something he'd detested as a kid.

Phin had never minded his full name—Phineas Ronald Theodore Younger —although it hadn't been the best name to have in school when you'd already been deemed the weird awkward kid.

Phin stared at the wedding invitation and the RSVP card enclosed inside. Ash had already asked Phin to be one of his groomsmen, but Phin guessed they'd sent the entire wedding party invitations regardless.

As Phin was about to fill it out and put only one person attending, he stopped himself. His family expected him to show up without a plus one, and normally, he wouldn't care that they'd expect this. But Katherine's words nipped at him. He growled under his breath and tossed the invite onto a nearby counter without filling it out.

Unbidden, he thought of Emily. It was stupid, but his brain latched onto the image and decided to follow it through. He saw Emily dressed in some gorgeous little black dress, heels on her dainty feet. Would she wear her hair up or down? He didn't know which would be more alluring—up, so he could imagine taking it down later that night, or already down, so he could run his fingers through it as they danced.

He swore under his breath. He wasn't going to ask a *client* to go to his brother's wedding. The wedding might be in two months, and maybe Josh's case would be over by then, but—

No, it wasn't worth thinking about. Emily wasn't the type of woman who'd want him, anyway. Phin didn't even resent that thought, because he'd long accepted that he wasn't the type of man women were generally attracted to. It was simply what life had given him, like his hair color or the fact that he was left-handed.

Thinking of Ash's wedding, Phin felt jealousy bloom inside him. What would it be like to have the love of a woman like Violet? Ash was damned lucky, that was for sure.

As Phin returned to his balcony, he finished watching the sunset until the sky turned a bruised purple with twilight. His mind circled around love, marriage, dating, Emily, and the fact that he already knew he wouldn't have any of those things.

CHAPTER FIVE

Emily stared at the words in her GED textbook and her head started pounding within moments. Squinting, she forced herself to concentrate, sounding out the words, only to realize that it had taken her over fifteen minutes to go through one page.

How was she going to get her GED at this rate when she could scarcely read the study materials?

Humiliation made her cheeks scarlet. This was why she studied at home, and this was the one instance where she was glad Josh wasn't here to see her struggle.

Oh God, I'm so selfish to think that! My little brother is in a detention center and I'm happy he's not here.

She rubbed her eyes, like it would somehow make the letters behave. It wasn't the longer words that tripped her up —sometimes it was the shorter ones, the ones that could be any number of words, like *won* or *now*. She hated homophones in particular: *there*, *their*, and *they're* were her mortal enemies. And when she was especially tired or anxious, her dyslexia seemed to get worse.

She blew out a breath. She'd wanted to get her GED for a number of years, but she'd had neither the time nor the ability to do it. As a child, she'd managed to get through school by being charming and pretty, and only one teacher had ever approached her mother about her possibly having a learning disability. She'd gotten some help in the fourth grade, but then her mother had had to move the family because they couldn't afford their apartment. This placed Emily and Josh in a new but poorer school district.

Emily's mother had done her best, and she didn't resent her mother for the fact that she could only read at a fourth-grade level. Besides, no one cared if a beautiful girl was smart. Emily's mouth twisted at the thought, but she was practical enough to acknowledge its truth.

Shortly after she'd dropped out of high school, a talent agent had spotted Emily at the local mall and had booked her for modeling gigs. It had been like some kind of fairy tale.

Emily had thought it would be her big break: she could make enough money to care for her ailing mother and her younger brother. But the darker side of the industry had eventually pushed Emily out of it. Now here she was, working as a waitress, trying to get her GED, and worrying herself to death over her teenage brother.

She glanced at her phone's clock. She had an hour before she would go see Josh in the detention center. He'd told her that she didn't have to visit him, but she was all he had. His so-called friends had deserted him the second they'd learned he'd been arrested.

Emily flipped to the math section of her study book. Math had always been easier for her than reading. She'd almost thought about becoming a math teacher when she'd been a kid, until life had beaten that dream out of her.

The thought of reading—and books, and school—inevitably made her think of Phin. She remembered all of the books in his office, the degrees in frames on the wall. What would he say if he saw her now, poring over a GED textbook? A man who'd passed the bar at only twenty-three? After some Internet sleuthing, Emily had discovered that Phin was not only well educated, but a prodigy of sorts. He'd even graduated from high school at sixteen, while Emily had dropped out at that age.

Time passed quickly as Emily did some algebra equations. She took her book with her to study on the bus ride to the detention center, about a thirty-minute ride. A man sat down next to her, and when he saw what she was doing, he said in a tone that was supposed to be encouraging, "I got my GED last year, but what's a pretty thing like you worrying about that for? If I were as pretty as you, none of that shit would matter."

He laughed as Emily ignored him. God, she was tired of people assuming that because she was pretty, she was also stupid. Sometimes it was hard not to believe them.

After Emily had gone through security at the detention center, she arrived at the waiting room, where a few other families were spending time with their kids. Josh sat at a table in the corner, his long legs outstretched, his arms crossed across his chest. He'd started growing a beard, and it only made Emily sad to see it. More and more, he no longer looked and acted like her little brother.

"How are you?" she asked as she leaned down and hugged him. He barely returned the gesture; her heart pinched.

"How do you think? Everything is shit," he said, his lip curling.

Emily sat down across from him, taking a deep breath. Torn between fear and frustration, she struggled to figure out how to talk to her brother. Should she reprimand him? Beg him to behave? Ignore him entirely? What did you do with a teenage boy who was too angry to listen to reason?

"You're lucky you aren't in prison. At least here you have some freedom," she said.

"I can't even take a shit without asking permission. How is that freedom?"

"I'd feel sorry for you if you hadn't broken the law," she snapped.

His mouth settled into a stubborn line. "I didn't do anything," he muttered. "Not like Reggie. This is all bullshit."

"Do you think if you say that enough times, the judge will suddenly agree with you?" Emily shook her head. "Josh, we can't help you if you refuse to help yourself. Phin is doing everything he can—"

"Who the hell is Phin?"

She blushed a little. "Your lawyer. Mr. Younger."

Josh sneered. "That guy? He looks like a total pansy. And everybody knows lawyers like him don't care about people like us."

Emily felt that headache from earlier start to return. "That doesn't mean he isn't working hard for *you*. The least you can do is be grateful."

"Grateful? Are you fucking kidding me?" Josh's voice rose, and a security guard stepped toward them. Emily shook her head. The guard stopped, although she knew very well that if Josh yelled again, this meeting was over.

Emily hissed, "Keep your voice down. Do you want me to leave? Because I will. I don't have to be here. But I'd like to remind you that I'm all you've got. None of your friends have come to see you, have they?"

Josh didn't reply.

"That's what I thought. And I know you. I know you're scared out of your mind."

"I'm not scared." But he didn't look at her as he said it.

She softened her voice. "You know what I was thinking about today? When Mom was still alive. Remember when she'd save up her money and take us to get ice cream at that place on the corner?"

Josh shrugged. "So what?"

"I think you were about five at the time. You always got Rocky Road on a sugar cone." Emily smiled at the memory. "I got butter pecan, and Mom got mint chocolate. It was a really hot day—I remember that. Hotter than it usually gets. Your ice cream started melting way too fast, and as we were walking out of the store, most of your ice cream fell off your cone onto the ground. You started bawling."

"Why are you talking about this?"

"I'm getting there. Well, Mom being Mom, she wasn't about to spend money on ice cream that melted seconds after we'd gotten it. She marched back into that shop and after some negotiation with the clerk, she got you another ice cream cone. I never knew how she paid for it. Maybe the guy just took pity on you. But that was Mom. She wouldn't let us down no matter what.

"When Mom died, I told myself I'd take care of you like she took care of us. I knew I could never replace her. I've tried my hardest, though. I hope you know that, except now I can't help but think I've failed you."

Josh sighed. "Now you're being stupid."

She smiled a little at that. "Maybe. But if you think I'm going to let you get lost in the system on my watch, you're wrong. You'll always be my baby brother who cried when his ice cream fell on the ground. I love you, Josh. Even when I want to strangle you."

Josh still wouldn't look at her, but Emily knew her brother well enough to see the lines softening in his face as he took in her words. Maybe she imagined it, but she could almost see her little brother underneath that mask of anger and defensiveness.

"How have you been spending your time?" she asked into the silence. "I've been studying for my GED. I hope you can finish up high school after this. You don't want to get behind."

Josh shrugged for the thousandth time. "Does it matter? I wasn't going to go to college anyway."

"You can't get a job anywhere without a high school diploma." Her mouth twisted. "Believe me, I know."

"You've done fine."

"Do you think waitressing until my feet are covered in blisters and scrabbling for tips is 'doing fine'? I want better for you than that. You should want better than that."

Josh finally looked at her. "What about you? You don't want better?"

"I do. That's why I want to get my GED."

"And how many times have you tried to get it? Three times?" The softness in his face disappeared within moments. "How many times until you finally give up?"

Emily stared at him in astonishment before anger took its place.

"If you're just going to be insulting, I have no reason to stay. I don't know what happened to my baby brother, but whoever he's become? I don't like him. At all. He's mean and he's hateful."

She stood up, her voice still low but hard. "If you keep this up, you'll end up in prison for real. Is that what you want? Because if you're convicted of a felony, you won't be able to get a job. You won't be able to vote, or get a loan, or do anything with that conviction hanging over you."

"Shit, Emily——"

"No, listen to me for once. Stop being so selfish. Think about what this is doing to *me*. Yes, me. I've worked my fingers to the bone to provide for you because I love you, but if you're just going to toss your life away for something this *stupid*, I don't want any part of it. Do you hear me? I don't have to visit you. I don't have to work with your attorney. I don't have to write letters to the judge about what a good kid you used to be——I don't have to do anything. I could let you get lost in the system and nobody would blame me."

Josh stared at her, as if he didn't know who she was anymore. *Good*, she thought. *Maybe he'll finally listen to me.*

But then that hardness returned to his expression, and he just shrugged. Shrugged! "Do what you want," he muttered. "I can take care of myself."

"Then I hope you have a lovely time in prison," she said scathingly.

When she got on the bus to return home, she stared at the floor, completely dazed. She almost missed her stop because her mind couldn't compute what had just happened. She wanted to go back and tell Josh—what? She was sorry? She wasn't sorry, because she'd spoken truthfully. But that didn't make it hurt any less.

Emily tossed her bag onto the counter when she arrived home, her GED textbook slipping out as if to mock her. In that moment, she felt the futility of everything she was trying to do when the universe seemed so against her. She'd never wanted a lot—just to be secure, to be loved. To take care of her brother. Was that too much to ask?

She took out the GED textbook, staring at the words that floated and danced on the cover. Rage filled her. In a fit of anger, she threw the book at the wall. She wished the wall were Josh's head, if only to knock some bit of sense into him.

CHAPTER SIX

Early as always, Phin waited outside the detention center and decided to call his brother Ash to waste time. He told himself he wasn't loitering outside so he could run into Emily, but it was a big, fat lie.

"Phin! I thought you were dead. Thanks for finally calling me back," said Ash with a laugh. "How's it going?"

Ash had called Phin three times in the last week to talk about getting Phin fitted for his tuxedo, but between three different clients and Katherine haunting his office with offhand comments about going on dates with various women she knew, Phin had completely forgotten to call his older brother back.

"Not dead," answered Phin dryly, "although I feel like I should be."

"Don't die before my wedding, because then we'll have an uneven number of bridesmaids to groomsmen and Violet will have a fit."

When Phin was younger, he would've taken Ash's comment at face value. It was only as he'd gotten older that he realized that most people tended to say the opposite of what they meant. It had puzzled him as a small child; now he merely used it to his own advantage.

"Can you come up next weekend? That seems to work the best for everyone," said Ash.

Right then, Emily came walking toward Phin, her dark hair in a pretty braid over her shoulder. She smiled brightly as she saw him. Phin's heart did that annoying little clench it always did when he saw her.

Which wouldn't be for much longer. Phin would have Josh take this plea deal to save his skin, and then it would be over. Phin would never see Emily or her brother again. He told himself that was how it should be.

"Were you waiting for me? Oh, you're on the phone. Sorry." Emily smiled awkwardly and was about to go inside, but Phin shook his head, stopping her.

"Ash, I have to go. Talk to you soon."

"Did I hear a woman's voice? Phin, are you holding out on me? Hey—"

Phin hung up before Ash could needle him. It was one of Ash's favorite pastimes.

"Just talking to my brother. How are you?" said Phin as he and Emily entered the center.

Her mouth turned down as they went through security. He suddenly felt the weight of the place right then. He was used to the guards, the metal detectors, the feeling that it was just one step above a prison for kids.

But seeing Emily's drawn expression, he realized how screwed up that was, that he was used to this by now. How all the adults in this place didn't bat an eyelash anymore. A feeling of futility washed over him in that moment, making him wonder why he even tried at all.

"Oh, I didn't answer your question," said Emily. She shrugged. "I'm fine. My brother is in here, and I can't raise enough money to bail him out, but at least he isn't in prison."

Phin wished he could offer platitudes, something to make her smile. He didn't have platitudes—he never did. Instead, he said rather gruffly, "He's lucky, your brother, considering what happened."

"Maybe. Or maybe he's just another cog in a wheel of this messed-up world, that chews up and spits out kids like him. And like me." She laughed a little. "I'm sorry. I'm talking about nothing."

"Not nothing. Because I was one of those kids, too."

Emily's eyes widened just slightly before she covered the reaction with a bland expression. "Then you know how easy it is to fall into this particular pit."

"Too well."

Emily seemed like she wanted to say something else, but right then, Josh's JCC—juvenile court counselor—took them to his office. Harry Benson wasn't much older than Phin himself, although the lines on his face and the grim set to his mouth made him seem much older. Phin had worked with Harry multiple times already, and Phin knew that the man did his best for the kids inside here, despite a constant lack of resources.

"Hello, Younger. Nice to see you again, Ms. Lassiter. Josh is with a tutor right now." Harry shook Phin's hand before shaking Emily's.

"Is he finally working on school again?" said Emily, hope in her voice. "He told me he thought it was a waste of time."

Harry smiled wryly. "There's not much to do around here except stare at the wall or try to keep up with school. Your brother finally decided he'd had enough wall-staring contests."

Harry's desk was always covered in paperwork; Phin was fairly certain Harry would never be able to finish it all at once. Photos of Harry's wife and son encircled his computer monitor, while one wall had a faded motivational poster on it that read *Perseverance—when the going gets tough, the tough get going*. When Phin had asked about it once, Harry had said it had been left by the last counselor, who'd quit because he couldn't do this job anymore. They'd both laughed darkly at the irony.

"I wanted to talk to you about an incident this morning," said Harry right as Phin and Emily sat down. "I'm sorry to say that Josh got into a fight with another one of the boys."

Emily paled. "A fight? Is he okay? Is the other boy okay? I'm so sorry, I told him to behave—"

Harry held up a hand. "Don't apologize for him, Ms. Lassiter. I saw the entire thing. In Josh's case, he was provoked: the other boy kept throwing bits of food at him. Your brother ignored it, until the other boy said something. I didn't hear what he said, but Josh suddenly got up and grabbed the other boy. It took me and another security guard to break them up."

Phin grimaced. Josh getting into a fight here wouldn't help his case one bit. The judge could easily say that he should be remanded to adult court.

Phin rubbed his temples as he said, "Was anyone seriously injured?"

"No, thankfully. The other kid got a black eye, while Josh has a split lip. I've seen way worse." Harry spoke directly to Emily now. "I'm sure you can guess that it doesn't help Josh to get into fights right now. He's already on the razor's edge with these charges against him. This could move his case to adult court."

To Emily's credit, she didn't burst into tears. Not like at Phin's office, when she'd looked so defeated and so haunted. She kept her back straight, her hands in her lap. Only Phin could see how her fingers trembled.

"I'll talk to him," she said, steel in her voice. "Because I'm not going to let him throw his life away, no matter how much he seems not to care about it."

Harry nodded. "I'll tell someone to bring Josh down to the meeting room. Are you going to discuss the plea deal?"

"Yes. I believe it's in everyone's best interests," said Phin.

He and Emily entered the meeting room, and Phin couldn't help but be reminded of a feral animal when he saw Josh. But not an animal that had been feral all its life. Once he'd been a cherished pet, cosseted and fed, but then shitty circumstances had forced him onto the streets, and he'd done what he had to do to survive.

Phin could see the fear in Josh's eyes, the uncertainty, which Josh covered up with a bad boy's bravado. While Phin had buried himself in his books to avoid real life, Josh had tried to avoid it by acting like he was above the law itself.

Josh didn't say anything as he and Emily sat down across from him. His lip was swollen, and there was a cut on his forehead.

"Oh, Josh," said Emily sadly. "What happened?"

He shrugged. "I don't want to talk about it."

"Well, you should. You realize that this could be used against you. What were you thinking, getting into a fight? How do you think the judge will look at this?"

"Do you really think it'll matter in the end?"

She looked shocked. "Of course it will. What are you talking about?"

Phin had seen this exact situation too many times: one person intent on their self-destruction, while another person did everything they could to save that person. Except more often than not, both people were destroyed in the end.

Phin said quietly, "If it doesn't matter, then why are you wasting my time? Because I have other clients who are more than willing to try harder than you are."

Surprise, then anger, crossed Josh's face. "You don't even fucking know me."

"No, but you're pretty much like any other teenage client I've had to deal with. The ones who think that if they act tough, they'll get through this without a scratch. That isn't how this works, though. The law doesn't care if you act tough. And to be honest, I have enough on my plate without wasting time with someone who thinks he knows better than his own lawyer."

Josh started to stand, like he wanted to fight Phin, too. Phin just waited. Josh was just a boy—an angry boy, but a kid nonetheless. He didn't scare Phin.

"Josh, sit down. For God's sake. Stop this. Can't you just shut up and listen to what someone else has to say for once?" said Emily.

At that, Josh sat down, but he crossed his arms and looked away, like he could ignore everything going on and it would go away.

If only life worked like that.

Phin leaned forward, his voice low. "If you want out of here at all, you need to keep yourself out of trouble. No, I don't care what some other kid says to you—turn around.

Walk away. Because if you get into another fight, you aren't leaving this place, and more than likely, will end up somewhere much worse."

"Is that supposed to scare me?" said Josh.

"It should. Have you ever been to a real prison?"

Josh glanced at Emily, but she just waited for his answer. Phin could tell that she was as frustrated with her brother as Phin was.

Finally, Josh admitted, "No."

"Then you don't know how you only get a certain number of phone calls to people outside every day. How you're told where to sleep, when you can go outside. You'll sleep in a dorm with other prisoners, no privacy, nothing. You'll have to save up money or hope someone outside is kind enough to send you money for anything you'd consider a basic luxury—soap, a razor. You'll never get a moment alone. You'll always have someone watching you."

Phin shook his head. "You're just a kid, no matter how much you want us to think otherwise. Don't toss your life away like this. You have the chance to turn things around. Don't keep going until it's too late."

Josh had turned pale, as if he'd never considered what prison would mean. He looked away again, but Phin could see the fear in his eyes. He could see the tension running through him. If Josh thought this place was hell, then he couldn't imagine real prison.

"Listen to him, Josh. If not for yourself, then for me. I know you can keep out of trouble," pleaded Emily.

Silence fell. Phin decided he might as well put everything on the table.

He said, "I'm advising that you take a plea deal, Josh. This means that you'll plead guilty to the lesser crime of second-degree theft, which means you'd probably just get probation. You also won't be tried as an adult." Phin took a deep breath, knowing the next words he said probably wouldn't go over well. "The plea deal is contingent, however, on you testifying against Reginald Berkley."

Josh's head swiveled toward him, his eyes wide with shock, then disgust. "I'm not going to rat out my best friend," he said. "What the fuck is wrong with you?"

"He's clearly not a great friend, considering he's apparently more than willing to rat *you* out."

"No. You're wrong. You're just saying that to get me to agree."

"Why would he lie? He has no reason to, Josh," said Emily.

"He's a lawyer. They're all liars."

Phin could see the stubborn look come back to Josh's face, and he wanted to shake the boy.

"I'm not ratting out a friend. Snitches get stitches," recited Josh.

"Oh, Josh," whispered Emily.

"Then I guess we're done here." Phin stood.

He waited for Emily, but she shook her head. "I want to talk to him in private."

Phin went outside again, leaning against the brick wall and feeling the sun beat down on his face. He didn't need to wait for Emily a second time. He knew that, and yet, he wanted to. He wanted to make sure she got on the bus okay. He wanted to—what? Talk to her? Do more than talk to her?

He laughed darkly. He pushed his fingers through his hair, disheveling it.

He made a few calls, almost about to leave, when Emily came outside finally. She started in surprise when she saw him.

"You didn't need to wait for me."

Phin stuffed his hands in his pockets. "I wanted to," he said gruffly.

Color suffused her cheeks. When she bit down on her lower lip, Phin almost groaned. Why did she have to affect him so much?

"Josh says he won't take the deal. I don't know what to do." Emily wrung her hands.

"It's his decision. Let him think about it."

She sighed. "I know, but he's so stubborn. I could see him refusing to do it just out of spite."

"Then he signs his own life away. That's his choice."

Emily looked so defeated right then, her shoulders slumped, dark circles under her eyes. Had she been sleeping at all? When she winced as she leaned against the same wall Phin had been standing against, he said, "What is it?"

"Oh, nothing. Just my arms. They're tired from working all night." She rubbed her right forearm, flexing her fingers.

Phin could see calluses on her palms and see the muscles in her arms from working hard. A white scar covered the back of her right thumb, and before he thought better of it, he lifted her hand to his face. "Burn?" he asked.

Her voice was breathy now. "Yeah, from the fryer. Got too close one night and paid for it."

He touched the scar with his thumb. Yet when Emily shuddered slightly, he let her go.

God, he was a fool. It didn't matter that she was beautiful and kind and devoted to her brother. It didn't matter that he wanted to touch the dark curl of hair that lay against her neck that had come loose from her braid. It didn't matter that he wished he could keep her safe somewhere, until the calluses faded from her hands and that she'd never get burned or hurt working again.

None of what he wanted mattered, though. All he could do was try his best to save her brother.

Phin knew that if Josh were lost, it would destroy Emily most of all.

CHAPTER SEVEN

For the first time in a while, Emily had been glad that the diner was busy. A football game had ended in victory, and it seemed like the entire city had emptied out of their homes into every bar available to celebrate. Now that it was edging toward midnight, people were drunk and hungry, which made Emily's place of work the perfect place for rowdy football fans.

Emily had already been pinched, asked out, and had her breasts stared at, but she was used to it. If she acted like a dimwit, usually the guys left her alone. If some guy got too handsy, Lawrence would take care of him.

And if not Lawrence, then Jenson would. Burly and taciturn, Jenson had worked as the cook at The Dine in Five for probably longer than Emily had been alive. Covered in tattoos, Emily had heard he'd been in jail for years, but she still didn't know why he'd been put behind bars.

"I need onions on this one," she said, pointing to the burger under the warmer.

Jenson grunted, lifting up the bun and slapping some

onions on top. A grunt from Jenson was generally all you got. Occasionally, if you were lucky, you'd get a rough "okay." Or, just a flat-out "no," depending on his mood.

"Thanks. How's Claudia?" Claudia was Jenson's girlfriend, who somehow managed to get actual whole sentences out of him.

"A pain in my ass," he muttered. He lifted his stubbled chin. "Take out that burger before it gets cold."

"Yes, sir." Emily saluted and carried the burger to the customer.

After serving the burger to her customer, Emily saw a lone man sit down at one of her tables. She froze when she realized who it was: Landon, her ex-boyfriend. What the hell was he doing here?

Landon hadn't stopped texting her about doing those nude photos for a nice sum of money, but Emily didn't want to do nude photos. She never had.

But things had changed, hadn't they? If she could get enough money, she could bail out Josh. And then he wouldn't get into any more fights, and maybe he could avoid real prison time.

"Hey, Emily," said Landon as she approached.

With his surfer boy looks and tan, Landon had smiled at Emily once, and she'd fallen for his spell. It wasn't that Landon was a bad guy; it was just that he'd been raised to get anything he wanted. He didn't understand why someone would tell him no, because it was rare that they did.

"Since when do you eat fast food?"

He grinned. "Since never. I'm here to see you."

She placed her notepad back into her apron pocket. "If you're not going to order—"

"I didn't say that." Landon waved a hand. "Get me a Diet Coke."

She almost told him that he was taking up a table that could have had real paying customers sitting at it, but she didn't have the energy. When she brought him his soda, he didn't even touch it.

"When do you get off?" he asked.

"Eventually."

He glanced at his watch. "Well, I know this place closes in an hour, so I'm going to assume you're off by then."

"What is this about, Landon? I have to work."

It almost amused her that he looked somewhat embarrassed by her tone. Then again, Landon was good at making people do things for him. He wasn't above wheedling and guilt-tripping.

"You won't return my texts. Come on, Em, this is a great opportunity, and you're the perfect girl for it." He glanced around the diner—at the faded wallpaper, the holes in the upholstery, the gum stuck under the tables—and added, "I know you need the money."

Emily's pride wasn't about to let her admit that to him, no matter how true it was.

"Meet me outside at one thirty," she said, caving.

Emily hoped that Landon would get bored and not wait for her, but to her surprise, he did. He even ordered a burger in the interim, although he only ate the patty. Landon had always been a health freak. When they'd been together, he'd tried veganism, making Emily do it, too. They'd both lasted all of three days on that diet.

At one thirty, Landon pointed to his car parked across the street. "Let's talk in private."

Normally, with any other guy, she would've balked. But strangely enough, despite his insistence that she do nude photos, she knew Landon wouldn't try anything. He was rather chivalrous, in an utterly selfish kind of way.

"You look good," he said when she got into the passenger seat.

The buttery leather seats made her want to curl up and take a nap. Her arms ached, her legs ached, and at that thought, she remembered how Phin had taken her hand, his thumb brushing across her burn scar. In that moment, she'd almost wished he would kiss her. Right outside the detention center, of all places.

That touch had been electric—and too brief. Phin had dropped her hand like she had the plague.

"And you want something," she said, pushing the memory of Phin away. "I already told you no."

"That's because you haven't heard me out yet. I've gotten a contract with this website that sells nude photos of girls. No, wait, let me finish. It's not a porn site—it's more an erotica site."

Emily snorted. "Isn't that the same thing?"

Landon almost looked affronted. "The photos I do are classy, Em. Artistic. And best of all, you get to keep a percentage of the royalties. It's not just one sum for taking them."

That was interesting, and Emily couldn't help but listen further. When Landon showed her photos of other girls, she admitted, "They are pretty. Naked, but pretty." When he swiped to a photo of a woman in a particularly *erotic* position, Emily blushed. "I can't take photos like that!"

He shrugged. "Why not? They're pretty tame, all things

considered. But don't forget that I can offer you a good sum of money upfront, not including royalties later."

Her mouth went dry. God, she needed the money. She needed it desperately. Enough to get Josh out of that detention center, to pay her rent, everything. What would it be like to make enough that she put some money away? She'd never done that before in her life.

"How much?" she whispered.

"Ten thousand upfront."

She gasped. She couldn't help it. She'd expected maybe one thousand, two if she was lucky. But ten thousand? She'd never had that much money at one time in her life. Ten thousand could free Josh. And then, if Landon was telling the truth, she could make serious cash after the photos were published.

But then that voice in her head, the one that was uncomfortable with doing full nudity, whispered in her brain. Her practical side knew it was silly to care about that, because desperate times called for desperate measures. And it wasn't just the nudity—it was the exposing herself for anyone to see. Any *man* to see. What happened if she tried to get a job somewhere and they saw those photos?

What would Phin think, if he saw them? She blushed scarlet at the thought, annoyed at herself. His opinion shouldn't matter to her, and yet, it did.

"What if I didn't do any of those, um, poses? The ones that show everything?"

Landon considered her. "The nudity is nonnegotiable."

"I know. I just mean that other stuff."

"Then I'd pay you half. They won't sell as well, I'll tell you that, but if you understand that—"

She nodded. "I'll do it, then."

Landon looked like he wanted to persuade her otherwise, but then he just shrugged. "Seems like a wasted opportunity to me, but it's your life. I'll send over the contract tomorrow morning. It'll have all the details in it."

Emily walked home after she'd said goodbye to Landon. She could've asked him for a ride, but she'd wanted time alone to think. Normally she took the bus, but talking to Landon had meant missing the last one. She didn't love walking around Portland at night, but generally there were enough people around to keep anyone intent on hurting a lone woman from trying anything.

A group of girls staggered out of a bar, laughing madly, one of them falling onto the sidewalk in a drunken sprawl. Emily looked away when the girl's skirt flipped up, revealing that the girl was definitely not wearing underwear. But the girl seemed too drunk to care, rolling around on the ground as her friends tried to help her up.

Had Emily ever been that carefree? She couldn't remember a time when she had been. She hadn't gone to college or partied with girlfriends, getting wasted and making stupid decisions. Emily had had to always make mature, thoughtful decisions, because she had to think of her brother, too. She had to keep food on the table, a roof over their head. She'd had to grow up before she'd understood what that really meant.

Her shoulders slumped as she walked. She didn't notice the guy following her until he started walking beside her. Emily's heart sped up as her feet sped up, too, but he just flashed her a grin and walked faster to keep up with her.

"Having a nice night?" he asked, like they were old friends.

The streetlights illuminated his face for a second before it was shadowed, and it only made a chill crawl down Emily's spine. She was at least three blocks from her apartment. Should she run? Scream? Or hope the guy was just messing with her and would let her be?

She ignored his question and walked faster.

"Hey, why the long face? Tell ole Donnie what's wrong. Somebody as pretty you shouldn't look so sad."

"Please leave me alone."

"I'm just being friendly. Let's get a drink. My treat. You look like you need it."

Emily turned and stopped so fast that Donnie almost tripped and fell on his face. "Leave me alone," she repeated. "I don't want a drink. I don't know you."

"You could. Come on, you know you want to—"

She kept walking and crossed the street. She wasn't about to take Donnie to her apartment. A block north, she saw lights spilling from a bar, and she hurried for it. If she could just get somewhere with people, Donnie would leave her be.

"Where you going?" Donnie caught her by her arm. She let out a surprised scream.

She ripped her arm free, darting around Donnie to the bar in question. Her heart hammered. By the time she reached the bar, she ripped open the door, glad that it was too seedy of a place to ask for ID. She almost ran into a guy playing pool. Muttering an apology, she found the bathroom —blessedly single occupant—and locked herself inside.

She leaned her forehead against the bathroom door, trying to catch her breath. She waited, listening for Donnie. When no one banged on the door, she wetted a paper towel with cold water, sponging her forehead.

Catching her reflection in the greasy mirror, she almost laughed: she was wild-eyed and deathly pale except for the color in her cheeks that was slowly fading after her impromptu sprint. Her mascara had turned to dark circles under her eyes, and she desperately needed to brush her tangled hair. Wiping the mascara from under her eyes, she knew this was a small thing she could control in a world that seemed terrifyingly chaotic.

"Hey, you dead in there?" a man shouted through the door. "I've been waiting forever!"

Emily gulped and unlocked the door to see a huge guy practically growling at her. He pushed past her into the restroom, slamming the door shut with a muttered *fucking women.*

She looked around for Donnie, but she didn't see him. Sighing deeply, she decided to order a cheap beer, mostly as penance for using the bathroom for so long.

"What's your cheapest beer?" she asked the bartender, sitting on one of the barstools.

"It's all cheap," the bartender replied, "because it all tastes like piss water."

That was quite a winning endorsement, Emily thought. She ordered a light beer that did, indeed, taste like piss water. But it cooled her parched throat, and as the alcohol filled her stomach, the tension in her limbs started to dissolve.

She rubbed her temples, exhaustion swamping her right then. She could fall asleep on this bar counter right then if she wasn't careful.

"You okay, lady?" the bartender said. He pushed a beer to

the one other man at the bar. "You want me to call somebody for you?"

She shook her head. "I don't have anyone you could call."

"A pretty lady like you? I doubt that."

"Believe it." She finished off her beer in one large gulp. "And beauty has never helped me get anywhere."

The bartender raised a dark brow, but he didn't comment on that. He pushed a refill to her, but when she protested, he just said, "On the house."

It was such a randomly kind gesture that Emily almost burst into tears. She sniffled, forcing the tears back, wishing she weren't such a hot mess. She drank her second beer without tasting it. She should go home, but she was terrified that Donnie would be lurking outside for her. She considered calling the cops, but Donnie hadn't threatened her. Not really.

She just wanted to feel safe. Secure. Was that too much to ask? She knew people felt that way, but she'd never experienced it in her life. Not since she'd been a child.

Was it too much to ask to feel like the world wasn't going to collapse on top of her with every breath she took?

"Ms. Lassiter?" a voice she'd recognize anywhere said in surprise. "Is that you?"

Emily turned to see Phin Younger standing in this seedy Portland bar, still immaculately dressed despite his lack of coat and tie.

Tipsy and exhausted, she blurted, "What the hell are *you* doing here?"

CHAPTER EIGHT

Phin stared at Emily before he realized that her question made sense, objectively, and that she seemed tipsy. How much had she had to drink?

She clapped a hand over her mouth. "Oh God, I'm sorry. That was so rude."

"It's a valid question, all things considered," he said, trying not to smile.

He wasn't exactly a bar hopper, but sometimes when he couldn't sleep, he'd come to Jackson's and have a drink, maybe play some darts. He liked to watch the people coming and going, watch the men play pool while their girlfriends tried to distract them. Phin could sit at a booth in the corner, no one caring how long he sat there as long as he bought a few beers. The noise and the movement kept his mind from obsessing about whatever it wanted to obsess about that day: his clients, his family. His own loneliness.

"I didn't think you knew what a bar was," said Emily. She blinked up at him. "Do you even drink?"

Yes, she's definitely tipsy, thought Phin. "Yes, I drink." He gestured to the barstool next to her. "May I sit down?"

"Okay." She seemed unsure, which Phin didn't understand. Had he made her uncomfortable when he'd touched her that last time? He winced inwardly. He knew better. He'd potentially jeopardized this case because he couldn't control himself.

But Emily didn't shy away from him. Instead, she put her cheek on her hand and said, "Do you live around here?"

"Not really." Which was true.

Her eyes narrowed. "Then you just drive over here to come to this place?" She waved a lazy hand. "Aren't there nicer places where you're at?"

"Not ones that stay open this late."

She frowned. Phin ordered his usual from Geoff the bartender, who had been watching Emily with a look that could be either interest or concern. Maybe both.

Given her delicate beauty, Phin could understand why men were drawn to Emily. He was one of them. She was like the princess in the tower, and he wanted to defeat the dragon guarding her and take her away on his horse.

It was a stupid thought. He scowled at his beer for a second, but long enough for Emily to notice.

"What's up with you, Mr. Lawyer Pants?"

Phin coughed. "Mr. Lawyer Pants? Really?"

"You didn't answer my question."

"And what about you? Why are you here alone? I've never seen you here before."

She shrugged, looking away. "I was walking home from work."

When she paused, he coaxed, "And…?"

"Some guy started following me. Bugging me."

At that confession, Phin's body tightened, anger racing through him. The feeling of protectiveness surprised him, it was so swift and sudden. The thought of some guy harassing Emily, even hurting her… it made him want to break things. Preferably the guy's face.

"Are you okay?" said Phin, trying to keep his tone modulated. "He didn't touch you, did he?"

"He grabbed my arm—" At Phin's low growl, her eyes widened. "But I got away. Ran in here. But I was too scared to see if he was waiting for me outside." She laughed sadly. "I guess I'll just have to live here now."

"I'll drive you home."

"What? No, you don't have to do that."

His tone was firm, implacable. "I don't have to, but I'm going to. Do you think I would let some guy hurt you if I could prevent it?"

She stared at him in surprise, and he suddenly felt uncomfortable for revealing so much to her. Hadn't he just told himself to get it together when it came to her? But when a softness came into her expression, and she touched his arm, he knew he'd never regret what he'd said. If it meant keeping Emily safe, he'd do anything.

"Okay, thank you," she whispered.

She played with a piece of her hair, which only made Phin want to touch her hair himself. It took all of his willpower to keep his hands to himself, especially when Emily looked up at him through her long, dark lashes. That look went straight to his groin. He took a drink of his beer in the hopes it would cool his ardor. He was just glad this place was dim, and Emily couldn't see how tight his slacks had become in the last five minutes.

"This doesn't seem like the type of place you'd hang out at," said Emily. She twisted that one piece of hair around her finger, let it go, and repeated the gesture.

Phin tore his gaze from that tendril with effort. "How do you know what type of place I'd hang out at?"

"Someplace nicer."

"Like I said, the nice places close early."

She frowned. "Still doesn't make sense."

"Am I that stuffy to you?"

She blushed a little. "No, I didn't mean that—I mean, kinda. You're so smart, and a lawyer, and you have degrees and books and everything."

Phin wasn't sure where she was going, so he just waited and listened.

"You have everything. And people who have things don't go to bars like this."

He struggled to understand what she really meant, something he'd had to learn how to do his entire life. She thought he had everything, when he could easily take her to his tiny apartment and show her otherwise. The thought of Emily in his apartment didn't help his pounding heartbeat, and he pushed the thought away with force.

"I don't have everything," he said slowly. "I'm a public defense lawyer. We hardly make millions."

At that, she flinched, and he didn't know why. He was speaking the truth. Why did people always flinch away from the truth?

"But you're smart. Really smart. I know you graduated

high school early." At his surprised look, she shrugged. "I Googled you."

He was so surprised that he couldn't find his voice for a long moment. But then he reminded himself she'd probably Googled him to figure out who was representing her little brother in court. Nothing more, nothing less. It made objective sense, even if his emotional side wished it were for some other reason.

"Sometimes I just like to go someplace where no one looks at me, or expects anything of me. I can come to this place and disappear for a few hours," said Phin quietly.

"I wish I could disappear sometimes, too." Her bottom lip wobbled. "But then who will be there for Josh? Except I can't even get enough money for his bail. I can get half, but where am I going to get another five thousand dollars?"

She looked so sad, so forlorn, that Phin wanted to cheer her up. He wasn't surprised she couldn't afford Josh's bail, but hearing it out loud depressed him nonetheless. He wasn't good at banter or jokes—that was his brother Ash's purview. Ash could make a sobbing woman smile with a grin and a sly phrase. Even Trent was better at that than Phin. Phin just had blunt honesty.

"I want another drink. Bartender!" Emily waved at Geoff. "Yoo-hoo!"

Considering there was all of one other person at the bar, Emily didn't need to yell. Phin stifled a laugh at the look on Geoff's face.

"I want another beer," said Emily decisively. "Can I get one?"

Geoff glanced at Phin, as if to ask, *You looking out for this chick?*

Phin nodded. He'd make sure Emily got home safely—that was something he could promise.

Emily drank half of her beer and laughed. "I feel so much better." She gasped as she turned. "Let's play darts!"

She grabbed Phin's arm, and Phin followed her over to the wall as she set her drink down on a rickety table and pulled the darts from the board. She giggled when she dropped a dart. It rolled under a table, and Phin got a full view of Emily's luscious ass as she bent down to grab it.

If Emily had been sent here to kill him, she was doing a great job of it.

Emily handed him all but one of the darts to hold. "Let's do best out of five. You ready for this?"

She threw the dart, which bounced off the wall—nowhere near the board—and they both watched the dart roll back toward Emily's feet.

"I'm usually good at darts," she said. She took another dart from Phin's hand and threw it. This time, the dart caught the very edge of the board before dropping to the ground.

This went on for the next three throws, and by the last one, Phin was biting his tongue in half to keep from laughing. Emily's cheeks were red, her chest heaving, and he didn't know if he wanted to laugh more than he wanted to kiss her.

"This game is rigged!" She tipped back her beer and took a long gulp before slamming it down onto the table. "The board kept moving!"

"I think that's the beer talking," said Phin seriously.

She shot him a look. "It's your turn, then. Show me I'm wrong."

Phin set his own beer down, placing all but one dart on the pool table nearby. He closed one eye. He remembered how Trent had taught Phin to play darts all those years ago. Phin was hardly an expert, but as he threw the dart, and it hit the circle right outside the bull's-eye, he smiled.

"You just got lucky." Emily crossed her arms. "Keep going."

Phin ended up hitting the bull's-eye twice, the other shots in the circle around it. When he smiled widely at Emily as he collected the darts, she huffed.

"Fine, maybe I have had too much to drink. Or maybe I lied about being good at darts."

Phin snorted. "Then we need to fix that. Put your drink down and come here."

Her eyes widened, but Phin had just enough to drink to ignore the voice in his head that said this was a bad idea. He didn't give a shit if it was a bad idea.

When Emily stood in front of him, only a few inches separating their bodies, his mind's objections disappeared.

Emily was half a head shorter than Phin, her long dark hair hanging over her shoulder, exposing the vulnerable nape of her neck. Dark hairs curled there, and Phin wanted to press a kiss right there, lick the pale skin, hear her gasp in surprise.

He gritted his teeth. If she pressed against him, she'd feel how hard he was just from her closeness. The last thing he wanted was to freak her out. For God's sake, she'd run into this bar because of some creep. He didn't want to be another creep for her to contend with.

"Turn sideways so your right foot is in front of you," said Phin. "Yes, and rest your weight on it. There you go. You'll then point your torso and arm toward the board. Now, raise your arm." After Emily had raised her arm, Phin readjusted her grip so she held the dart with three fingers. "You don't want to hold it too tightly. Otherwise your throw will be way off."

Emily nodded. Her expression was so serious as she listened to his instructions that Phin couldn't help but think of how adorable she was. Most women would be giggling and not caring about what he said. Emily, though? She wanted to learn, and he could always appreciate that in a person.

"You'll want to aim upward slightly. Dart throwing goes along a parabolic curve," said Phin.

"A what?"

"As opposed to a straight line. It's like one half of a curve of a circle. Does that make sense?"

Emily nodded. *God, why is she so adorable?* he thought despairingly.

"Use the tip of the dart as your line of sight, which will be what you use to aim." Phin realized that Emily's eyes were starting to glaze over from his instructions, so he stood back and said, "Don't move anything but your arm and wrist when you throw. Now, try it."

Emily threw the dart, and it bounced off the board onto the floor.

Phin handed her another dart. He touched her arm, showing her the motion of throwing. As he did so, the side of his arm brushed her breast, and she stiffened. He let her arm drop, feeling like some kind of lecher.

"Try again," he said, trying not to sound too gruff.

After a few more tries, Emily managed to hit the board instead of the wall around it. When her dart landed in the circle closest to the bulls-eye, she squealed.

"I did it! Look, I hit the dartboard!"

To Phin's shock, Emily threw herself into his arms,

hugging him like he'd given her a car for her sixteenth birth-day. Nonplussed but unwilling to let this moment pass, he hugged her back. She smelled amazing, and Phin wished he could tilt her head back and kiss her right then and there.

To his surprise, she did tilt her head back to look up at him. When she licked her lips, that movement shot straight to his groin. The noise of the dive bar faded away, and every thought except Emily being in his arms fled Phin's mind.

He cupped her cheek. Her eyes widened.

And then somebody bumped into Phin, mumbling "sorry, man" as he passed by. The moment broken, Phin let Emily go.

What the hell was he doing, almost kissing his client in some dive bar? And when she was obviously tipsy?

"I should get you home," he said. "It's late."

"Oh. Okay. Thanks."

Phin told himself that Emily was silent on the ride to her apartment because she was tired, but he knew better. He almost apologized, but that would only make things worse. Because he didn't want her to think he didn't want her. He also didn't want her to think he *did* want her.

What a mess he'd gotten himself into.

"This is it," said Emily, pointing.

Phin parked on the street, squinting at the run-down building with trash scattered in front of it. Cats screeched nearby, while something that looked like a raccoon riffled through the bags of trash. A homeless man was curled up near the stairs to the building.

Emily lived here alone?

It's none of your business. She's a client.

"I'll walk you inside," he found himself saying.

He walked her to her door, one that was clean but worn

like the rest of the complex. One of the numbers on Emily's door was missing. Phin heard shouting in a nearby apartment, and then the sound of something breaking.

"Thank you for tonight," said Emily. She jangled her keys, clearly agitated.

Phin put his hands in his pockets, mostly so he wouldn't touch her again. "Of course. I'd do it the same for any woman."

Emily's face fell, and Phin immediately regretted his words.

"Well, good night." Emily unlocked her door and was about to go inside when Phin stopped her.

"You can call me anytime you need me." *Why am I saying this?* Suddenly, he didn't care about the reasons why. "Are you sure you'll be okay here?"

She blinked. "At my apartment? Yes."

Phin wanted to offer to stay with her, to protect her, to keep her from any harm. It was a primal reaction, one he'd always considered ridiculous. But this woman turned him inside out.

He nodded stiffly. To his surprise, Emily reached out and touched his arm before clasping his hand.

"You're a good guy, Mr. Younger. Better than any I've met in a long time."

"Phin," he said, his voice low.

"Phin, then." Her voice was a thready whisper.

The clasp of their hands bolstered him. He moved his hand so it gripped her arm, and then she was in his arms again. She didn't pull away, and for that, he thanked the universe.

Because he was going to kiss Emily Lassiter, and damn the consequences.

When his lips touched hers, she gasped, the sound quickly turning to a soft moan. That sound heated his blood as he kissed her. He reveled in the softness of her lips and the way she melted against him. She was all softness and light, and he wished he could keep her safe from everything in this life that could hurt her. He kissed her until she wrapped her arms around his neck and kissed him back with an ardor only matched by his own.

Someone yelled, reminding Phin of where they were. He ended the kiss with reluctance, especially as he took in Emily's red cheeks and lips.

The yelling brought clarity to his hazy mind. What was he doing, kissing his client in the middle of the night like this? Grimacing, disgusted with himself, he set her away from him through sheer force of will.

"I'll talk to you later." He turned before she could even reply.

He hated doing this to her, this hot-and-cold act. But he couldn't let this happen again. His career was on the line. Not only that, but Emily's brother's life was on the line, too.

If Phin's behavior were somehow made public, Phin could be removed from the case. And then what? Would Josh get remanded to adult court because no one else wanted to touch a case that was now tainted?

I need to let her go, Phin said over and over again as he drove home. *No matter how much I don't want to.*

CHAPTER NINE

That weekend, Emily showed up at Landon's studio and posed for the nude photos. They were all tasteful, as Landon had promised, but Emily couldn't help feeling like she'd sold herself out.

She posed behind a sheet that just barely covered her breasts. She couldn't help but think of the modeling jobs she used to get.

She'd gotten lucky in the beginning, snagging the attention of a famous photographer who was able to get her into major magazines for a variety of fashion spreads. Emily remembered how shocked she'd been when she'd seen the luxurious couture garments hanging on the racks, wondering if she'd be thrown out the door if anyone realized who she was.

Emily had loved modeling, but that world had almost destroyed her. She'd gotten dangerously thin, to the point that she'd gotten pneumonia one winter. After that scare, she'd had to cut all ties with the industry, no matter how well it paid. It wasn't worth killing herself.

"Good, good," said Landon as he clicked his camera.

"Look over your shoulder at me. Don't smile, but look like you're thinking of your lover." He chuckled, probably thinking she'd imagine him.

But right then, Emily thought of Phin Younger and how he'd kissed her outside her apartment just a few nights ago. Her body tingled, her pupils dilating without her realizing it.

Had she really kissed her brother's lawyer? The man who was so out of her league that it was laughable? The man she'd run into in some sleazy dive bar and who'd made sure she'd gotten home safely? Emily still couldn't believe any of that had happened. And he'd shown her how to play darts, the hard planes of his body pressed against her, the woodsy scent of him enveloping her senses.

Then that kiss… it had consumed her. She'd never wanted it to end. Despite his suits and his books and his degrees, Phin Younger knew how to kiss a woman. But then he'd basically pushed her away afterward.

Emily was in knots over Phin despite knowing there was no way the two of them could ever work out. A fish and a bird could fall in love, but where would they live? She was practical enough not to wish for impossible things.

After the photoshoot ended, Landon showed her the photos on his camera. Emily almost didn't recognize herself as she paged through them. She looked…sultry. Sensual. And completely unlike herself.

"Five thousand, as promised," said Landon as he handed her a check. "Don't spend it all in one place." He winked, and Emily rolled her eyes. She'd forgotten what a cheeseball her ex-boyfriend could be.

But the five thousand in her hand still wasn't enough to get Josh out of that detention center. Where would she get the other half? Her heart fell as she took the bus to work later that evening after depositing Landon's check in her very empty bank account.

Should she do another photoshoot? But who did she know who could book her work immediately? She hadn't spoken with any of her modeling contacts since she'd quit. And her agent had been so pissed at her for throwing everything away, he'd basically blackballed her from the industry.

Emily could barely concentrate at work that night, she was so distracted thinking about coming up with a way to get that second five thousand. She almost dumped a soda in one customer's lap, while another complained that she'd forgotten to include his order of onion rings.

Lawrence took Emily aside during her break to ask, "You all right, kid?" Lawrence knew about Josh's legal troubles, although Emily hadn't told him the extent of it.

She gave him a wobbly smile. "No, but I'll survive."

Lawrence sighed. "And that's it? Just surviving? That's no way to live life."

She almost considered asking Lawrence for a loan, but she knew this diner of his wasn't exactly making him rich, either. And he had his own family to care for. Besides, Emily had too much pride to beg for charity from her boss.

"I'm just in a rough spot right now," she said, "but I'll get through it. Both me and Josh. Things can only get better, right?"

Lawrence looked skeptical, but he was smart enough not to say it aloud.

The next morning, Emily had almost decided to call Landon to book another gig. She didn't know if he'd even say yes, but she didn't know what else to do.

As she sipped her lukewarm coffee, staring at the beige wall of her living room, she checked her email. An email from someone she didn't know was at the top, and when Emily opened it her, her eyes widened with shock.

My name is Violet Fielding, and I own a jewelry business. I got your number from a modeling agency, and I wanted to inquire about your rates and availability. Based on my discussion with my photographer, we would pay you upward of $5000 for your time.

Please let me know if you're interested. Phone or email is fine.

Emily almost dropped her cup of coffee onto the floor. What kind of serendipitous angel had sent her this email? It was too good to be true. It had to be spam. And what modeling agency? Emily hadn't been an official model for a few years now. Then again, she could still be on someone's books that this Violet had found her.

Emily dialed the number Violet had provided in the email, expecting to get some robo-message about a payday loan, but to Emily's surprise, a real woman picked up. A woman who owned a flourishing jewelry business in Washington and who needed a model.

When Emily put her phone down, the gig booked, she started laughing. Because now she could get Josh out of the detention center, and maybe, just maybe, keep him out of jail for good.

EMILY GLANCED at the address in her email and looked up at the building in question. Violet had asked Emily to do the photoshoot in Seattle, and when Emily had admitted she couldn't afford to travel that far, Violet had paid for her train ride without asking questions.

Emily took a deep breath and entered the nondescript building in downtown Seattle. She'd researched Violet's business and was fairly certain this was legit, but the suspicious part of her brain still wondered if this was too good to be true. And it had landed in her lap right when she'd needed it. The universe had never been that kind to her.

Entering a suite of offices, Emily rounded a corner to see a tall blond woman talking with a man.

"Oh, you must be Emily!" said the blond. "Let me know when you're ready and I'll take Emily down the hall," she said to the man, who must be the photographer.

The photographer departing, the blond held out her hand to Emily with a bright smile. "I'm Violet. I'm so glad you could do this, especially on such short notice. Did you have a nice train ride up here?"

Violet wasn't model gorgeous, but she had a girl-next-door look about her that made Emily want to smile. Emily shook her hand warmly. "Yes, and thank you for paying for it."

Violet waved a hand. "No problem. Jeremy is finishing up whatever it is he needs to do and then we'll get started."

Emily couldn't help but notice the large diamond on Violet's hand that sparkled under the lights. "Your ring is beautiful," she said.

"Thank you." Violet smiled down at her hand. "I told my fiancé I didn't need a huge ring, so he bought the biggest one he could find." She rolled her eyes, but Emily could see the happiness in Violet's face. "We're getting married soon, too. I told my fiancé that he could buy me a big ring but not pay for a giant wedding. He agreed with that, if you can believe it."

Emily smiled, wishing for a brief moment that she had the same kind of excitement in her life as Violet. Not just excitement—obvious love. Violet's fiancé wasn't even present, and yet Emily knew without a doubt that they must adore each other.

The photoshoot was held in a room draped in dark fabric. A stylist came to dress Emily while another did her hair and makeup. It wasn't as extensive as when Emily had modeled for fashion magazines, but Emily found herself enjoying herself as she was primped and made up.

When she looked at herself in the mirror later, she marveled at her transformation. The makeup wasn't heavy, the hair was pretty and sweet, but she looked like an idealized version of herself. Nobody looking at her would know that she had a younger brother awaiting trial for a crime that could put him behind bars for a long time.

"So, I want to make sure we focus on the jewelry," said Violet. She showed Emily the pieces she was going to model. "Some photos will have your face in them, but others won't. Luckily, you have lovely hands and arms, so I'm not too worried about not liking any faceless photos."

Although Emily had modeled clothing more than jewelry, she still knew how to give the pieces center stage. She modeled a necklace made of jade and rose gold that came together below her clavicle before a small piece dangled between her cleavage. Emily almost couldn't believe that Violet had made all of the jewelry herself, it was so stunning.

Next were two bracelets, then multiple sets of earrings and rings. More necklaces followed, and by the time the shoot was over, Emily wished she could spend part of the five thousand on buying some of the jewelry for herself.

But she had Josh to think about. With this check, she could get him out of that place. If she could just keep him close, maybe she could stop him from destroying his own life.

"Thanks again for doing this," said Violet after the shoot had finished. "I'd been looking for a good model for what felt like forever. I couldn't believe that Phin of all people knew of the perfect person."

Emily stilled. *Phin. Violet knows Phin?* For a wild moment, Emily wondered if Phin was Violet's fiancé but then dismissed the idea. Phin was too honorable to kiss another woman when he was engaged to another.

Emily must've looked shocked, because Violet frowned. "He didn't tell you? He said he would." She let out an annoyed breath. "Those Younger men. I swear. Phin is my fiancé's younger brother. Soon to be my brother-in-law."

Emily couldn't wrap her head around this information. Phin had set this up? Why? It made no sense.

She remembered vaguely telling him that night at Jackson's about how she couldn't afford Josh's bail, but in her drunken haze she'd forgotten about it. She'd never expected him to do this for her. It was too much. And then she wondered—what would she owe him in return for this huge favor?

"You look like you're going to faint. Here, let me get you a glass of water." Violet ushered Emily to a nearby chair before handing her a cold glass of water. "I'm sorry, I honestly thought you knew. I wouldn't have sprung that on you like that, although it really was just a passing comment by Phin."

Emily shook her head. "I was just surprised," she rasped. She sipped the water, hoping it would calm her pounding heart.

She couldn't read too much into this, whether good or bad. Phin said he wanted to help people, and he'd known she'd been a model. That was all. He probably hadn't thought beyond that.

"Ms. Fielding," said Emily.

"Call me Violet. I'm not that old yet." She winked.

"Violet—I'm just… why would Phin do this? He's my brother's lawyer." *And the man you kissed outside your door.*

Violet was silent a long moment, and Emily barely restrained herself from squirming.

"I'll admit I don't know Phin very well. He's an enigma to most of the family. Ash says that Phin has always kept himself apart, but I also know that he's a good man. So whatever his motive, I can't believe it to be anything but wanting to help."

For a strange reason, Emily wished his motives weren't pure. She could deal with a man wanting to make her beholden to him. Because if that were the case, she could break off this *thing* that was between them without a backward glance.

But how could she not fall for him even harder knowing that he'd helped her when she'd been desperate? Even worse, he'd done it without outright giving her the money himself. He'd given her a job, something honest where she could earn the money herself.

Tears clogged her throat. *What are you doing to me, Phin? This isn't helping me let you go at all!*

Violet patted Emily's knee. "I don't know what's going on between you and Phin, and although I'm totally nosy and would love to know the details, I won't ask. But I hope that you can be the woman to draw Phin out of his shell. And he clearly sees something in you, which, for a man like him, is a huge compliment."

Emily laughed sadly. "I thought you didn't know him well?"

"I don't, but Ash does, and he talked my ear off after I'd told him that Phin had suggested you as a model. I hadn't even called Phin to talk about models—I was calling about wedding stuff. When I told Ash, you could've knocked him over with a feather."

On the train ride back to Portland, Emily stared out the window, her mind in knots. She heard Violet's words over and over again, and Emily's treacherous heart beat faster when she imagined Phin's face. His kiss.

But she also knew they were so different that she would be wise to let him go. He didn't need a girlfriend who couldn't even read. He needed a girlfriend as smart and as educated as he was. He'd get bored with Emily as soon as he realized how stupid she was.

But that didn't stop her heart from thrilling each time she remembered how he'd gone out of his way to help her.

CHAPTER TEN

Phin set down his office phone receiver with a gratified sigh. Apparently Josh Lassiter had finally posted bail and been released.

When he'd contacted Violet about giving Emily a job, he hadn't told her any specifics. Violet, despite her intense curiosity, had agreed to look into it. So, Violet must have hired Emily for a job, and Phin couldn't help but be glad that he'd found a way to help her.

Of course, he had no intention of telling her of his connection to Violet. There was no reason Emily needed to know. Just knowing he helped her was enough for him, and now, her brother was out of the detention center.

And if he were honest, he'd admit that he hadn't stopped thinking about that damn kiss since he'd dropped Emily off at her apartment. He'd dreamt of it, over and over again. In some of the dreams, he'd picked Emily up in his arms and taken her inside before the kiss had turned into something much more interesting.

He gritted his teeth, telling his body to calm down. He

already knew he couldn't pursue Emily. This job with Violet was his last hurrah, the last way he could help her beyond getting her stubborn little brother to agree to this plea deal.

Phin buried himself in his work, working on other clients' cases, but inevitably, the strangest things made him think of Emily. A similar name in a file; the sound of a woman's laugh in the hallway outside his office door; the ring on Katherine's finger, reminding him of the job he'd gotten for Emily. He could just imagine how beautiful she'd looked wearing Violet's jewelry. Right then, he wished he could've seen her in person.

Katherine cleared her throat. "Are you in there?" she asked with a small laugh.

Phin started. "What?"

"I said, I have the completed documents for the Daniels case. You wanted them today, right?"

"Yes, I did. Thank you."

Phin tried to take the folder from Katherine, but she wouldn't let it go. She raised an eyebrow at him.

"I haven't seen you this distracted since…" She thought a moment. "I don't even know, actually. You're never distracted. It's always been kind of eerie."

Phin pulled the file from her grip. "I have a lot of work to get done."

"I heard that teenager you're working with had his bail posted. I'm surprised, given how high it was. Most of our clients could never raise that kind of cash. Hell, even I couldn't."

Phin waited, keeping his features a smooth mask. "And your point?"

"I don't have one. Just being gossipy. But I'm sure it's a

relief to the kid's sister. The gorgeous model woman." Katherine smiled slowly, as if she'd caught Phin in her net.

Phin didn't have time for Katherine's speculations. "Ms. Lassiter posted bail for her brother, yes. That's all I know at this point. I would imagine family or friends helped her. I didn't think to ask. Now, do you have anything you need from me? I have work to do, like I said."

Katherine looked disappointed at his reply. She opened her mouth, but then just shook her head without saying anything.

Phin didn't care to interpret that reaction from his friend and coworker. If Katherine thought he was wrong for avoiding an entanglement with a client, then Katherine was off her rocker.

Blowing out a breath, Phin flipped through the file Katherine had brought him, but he could barely concentrate. All he could see was Emily—her laugh as he showed her how to play darts. Her eyes widening right before he kissed her. The way she'd responded to him, like she could've stayed in his embrace forever.

Phin's phone rang. "Yes?" he barked.

"A client is here to see you," said Tammy, the front desk woman. "She doesn't have an appointment, but if you're not busy—"

"Who is it?" Phin said distractedly.

"Emily Lassiter."

Phin stilled. His heart pounding, he forced the excitement down as he replied, "Send her in. Thank you."

When Emily walked into his office, he drank in the sight of her. Today her hair was down, curling past her shoulders, and she blushed a little as she walked up to him.

"Ms. Lassiter, what can I do for you? Please, sit."

Emily clutched her purse. "No, I'm okay. I just wanted to come in person to thank you for what you did."

"What I did…?"

"The modeling job with your sister-in-law. I had no idea you would do such a thing to help me post Josh's bail. You can't know how much I appreciated it. And Josh, too. It was above and beyond. I can't begin to repay you."

Phin stared at her. How had she figured out the connection? Stupidly, Phin had assumed Violet wouldn't mention him to Emily, because he had made no intimation that he knew Emily personally. Clearly, he'd miscalculated.

Embarrassed and unsure how to proceed, he cleared his throat and tried to figure out a plausible excuse. "Violet had been mentioning needing a model," he finally said, all nonchalance. "I thought of you. That's all. She made the decision to hire you."

"But without you doing that…" Emily shook her head. "I thought it had to be too good to be true, but it wasn't. How often does that happen?"

Phin wanted to say that in his experience, things that seemed too good to be true were always just that—false and hollow. The fact that Emily ascribed such virtues to him—that she didn't assume he had some ulterior motive… he didn't deserve her trust, or the look on her face that spoke of untold gratitude.

Phin didn't want to be worshiped as a hero when he knew all too well that he was purely human and full of faults and weaknesses.

"Like I said, all I did was make the connection. Don't make more of it than it was," he said.

Emily cocked her head to the side, and Phin couldn't help but feel like she was trying to understand his very soul. "You don't like compliments, do you?"

"No," he deadpanned.

She smiled. "I can tell." She sat down in the chair in front of his desk with a thoughtful look on her face. "Most people who receive compliments say something like 'thank you.'"

"Aren't you the one thanking me?"

"True. Then it's not a compliment, but me being grateful. It's funny to me, considering the work you do, that you don't know what to do when people express gratitude toward you."

Phin didn't know what her game was. Was it to unsettle him? Make him regret helping her? Based on her expression, she seemed sincere, but Phin wasn't sure he could trust his own conclusions anymore.

"I'm grateful that you helped me and Josh," continued Emily. "I have a feeling you've helped more people than you know."

"It's my job to help people."

"Yes, but in other ways. In ways that people don't realize. You didn't want me to know what you'd done for me, right?" She shook her head. "I don't think I've ever met someone who does good things just because they're good."

Phin felt a blush climbing up his cheeks. He'd never met someone so honest with her feelings. He'd always considered himself frank to the point of sometimes offending people, but Emily didn't hesitate to speak what she felt. It was an admirable quality.

"How is your brother doing?" he asked, desperately wanting to change the subject. "Is he home now?"

"He's doing okay. He's still really angry, and when I called the detention center to tell him that I'd posted his bail, he didn't react like I'd hoped."

"He wasn't happy to get out?"

She shook her head. "It wasn't that. I mean, I don't know. He just acted like I'd done something stupid, and he refused to speak to me the entire ride home."

Phin rather wished he could take Josh out back and tell him how much of an asshole he was being to his sister. He might have the right to his anger, but he didn't have a right to take it out on his sister, who'd worked so hard to get him out.

"I just hope that, now that he's not in that environment, he'll behave. I asked him about the plea deal you talked to him about, but he said he still wouldn't do it," said Emily.

Phin leaned back in his chair. "He's still being stubborn, yes. I can't beg him to do what I think is best. If he wants to take this trial, then that's his right."

"Oh, what a mess!" Emily rose and went to stand in front of Phin's bookshelf, like she could find the answers to her brother in the titles. She turned back to Phin, her arms crossed. "I'm sorry he's so difficult. That can't be helpful for you when you have other things to deal with."

Phin marveled that she'd apologize to *him* when he could argue she'd been more wronged than him. Josh was simply another client to him at the end of the day, and he had no emotional involvement in the kid's life other than that. But Emily loved her brother—despite everything—and Josh couldn't even express gratitude for her actions.

Gratitude seems to be the topic of the day, thought Phin wryly.

"Don't apologize to me," he said, meaning it. "I'll do my best to convince him to take the plea deal. Just keep him from doing anything totally stupid. We don't need him getting into another fight."

"I'll try, but Josh is a wild card. He has been for a few years now."

Emily sighed, turning back to Phin's bookshelf. Phin could stare at her openly now: the curve of her back, the way her hair brushed her shoulders, the way she'd crossed her arms over her chest. She was so slight that he marveled that she could carry such burdens without collapsing. He almost rose to go to her, to take her in his arms, but he clutched his pen until it bit into his palm to restrain himself.

Emily wasn't his to protect, no matter how much he wanted to make himself that person.

"Have you read all of these books?" said Emily as she wandered down the line of his bookshelf.

"Most of them, or at least parts of them for different cases."

"I don't think I've ever seen someone have this many books of their own."

"I like to read," he admitted, as if it weren't already obvious.

She smiled back at him. "I can tell." She touched the binding of one book, her pale fingers in contrast to the dark brown leather binding. "Are they all law books?"

"Mostly, yes."

Phin got up to stand next to her. He pulled one book from the shelf, an old textbook from his law school days. He flipped through and smiled as he read the pencil scribbling in the margins.

But his attention was diverted when he realized how close he was to Emily, how her cheeks flushed at his nearness. He thought of their kiss and he almost gave in to temptation and kissed her. Here, in his office.

Emily gazed up at him, as if she, too, wanted him to kiss her. Phin couldn't help but touch a tendril of her soft, dark hair that lay near her collarbone. He fingered the silken strand, watching her reaction. She inhaled a sharp breath, but she didn't push him away.

"Emily," he said in a low voice.

"Yes?" Her voice was nothing but a breathy whisper.

He was about to lean down to kiss her, to feel her plush lips against his own a second time… but a knock on his office door effectively shattered the moment. Emily jumped away from him like a startled deer.

"Phin, I have that document for you," said Tammy through the door.

Phin went and opened the door. "Thank you. Since Ms. Lassiter is here, we can have her sign it now." He pointed to Emily, who hadn't moved from her station at his bookshelf.

Tammy hustled to Phin's desk, beckoning at Emily. "I need you to look over this first, if you have a moment."

Emily glanced at Phin, like she was unsure, but then she did as Tammy asked. Phin had a feeling Emily was still unsettled by their almost kiss, which was why she kept glancing over her shoulder at him.

"Although this is in regard to your brother," Tammy was saying, "since you're his legal guardian, we need your approval. I'll give you a moment to read through it."

Tammy left after Phin agreed to bring her the document when Emily finished. Phin sat down at his desk as Emily read the form. Her forehead was creased and she kept chewing on her lip.

"Is there something the matter?" he asked. At her startled look, he gestured at the form. "In the document, I mean."

"Oh, no. It's fine. Where do I sign?"

"On the line that says legal guardian. You don't need to sign any of the other lines. Those are for me."

Phin was now looking at the folder Katherine had brought him as he waited for Emily. Every once in a while, he looked at her from the corner of his eye, wondering why she seemed so out of sorts. Should he apologize for that kiss?

It was on the tip of his tongue to say something when she hurriedly rose and pushed the signed form to him.

"I'll see you later?" she asked, almost too brightly. "Have a great afternoon."

It was only after Emily had scurried out of his office that Phin glanced at the form she'd signed. He frowned when he saw that she'd signed the wrong line, the one that said *Attorney*. She really must've been distracted if she'd not heard his basic instructions.

Her signature was also odd to his eyes. It wasn't that it was messy, as most signatures were. It just seemed written in handwriting that was similar to a child's, like the writer had had to struggle to remember the correct letters.

Phin rubbed his temples. He'd need to get Emily's signature again, since she'd signed the wrong line. Something also niggled in the back of his mind, making him wonder, but he pushed it out of his head.

He had too much work to do to wonder about this particular mystery, which might be nothing at all to begin with.

CHAPTER ELEVEN

Two weeks after Josh had gotten out of the detention center, Emily almost wished she hadn't paid his bail. He was sulky, angry, and he didn't care about anything. He'd been frustrating before he'd been arrested, but Emily didn't recognize this Josh at all. When she pressed him about what had happened during his stay at the center, he got this tight-lipped look on his face and refused to answer the question.

That morning during her shift at the diner, she dreamed of going home early and taking a nap. Or sleeping for twelve hours. She'd lain awake all last night, tossing and turning, worrying herself to death about her brother.

And then when her thoughts decided they needed something new to agonize over, she thought of Phin Younger, and how stupid she'd felt leaving his office that afternoon.

Had he figured out that she couldn't read? That when he'd told her to sign that line that said *legal guardian*, she'd frozen like a rabbit in front of the barrel of a gun? She'd sat in his chair, cold sweat breaking out on her forehead, praying that her brain could figure out which line to sign on. But anxiety always made her dyslexia worse, and she'd decided to choose one random line and hope for the best.

Emily had gone home, humiliated and disheartened. Only moments earlier, Phin had looked like he'd wanted to kiss her a second time. He'd helped her get enough money to post her brother's bail. He obviously cared…but that didn't mean he would want a woman like her in his life.

He wouldn't want a partner who couldn't even read. She knew that with a cold practicality that cut through any feelings that she'd already developed for the aloof lawyer who'd touched her heart without seemingly trying.

Emily set down sodas for one of her tables right as Landon walked into the diner.

"Emily!" he waved, all smiles.

Emily gritted her teeth, not particularly wanting to deal with her ex-boyfriend right now. But when Landon sat down at one of her booths like he'd done that night weeks ago, she found herself once again taking his order.

"Is this going to become a habit with you?" she said.

Landon's white teeth flashed. "It's the only way I can talk to you. I texted you, but you ignored me. Or is your phone always off? I can never tell."

Emily tapped her foot. "Either order or I'm going to go back to work."

"You're in a mood. Well, I have good news. Those photos you took? They've been the most popular on the site in ages. The site has gotten so much traffic that it went down more than once. The servers couldn't handle it. Great, right? So I wanted to talk to you about doing some more photos."

"Landon, I don't have time right now—"

"Can't you take your break now?"

She rolled her eyes, but she couldn't help being curious. "When this table is done, I can talk and take my break."

A half hour later, she slid into the booth opposite Landon, stretching her aching calves under the table.

"I want you to pose for me again," said Landon without preamble. "But completely nude this time. None of this covered-up-with-a-sheet stuff."

Emily's heart pounded in her ears. "For how much?"

"Fifteen thousand."

Her jaw dropped. "You can't be serious. Are you joking?"

"No, I'm not." Landon leaned toward her. "I told you, your photos have exploded. If you went all the way, you could make serious royalties, not what you're getting now, plus triple what I paid you before. So what do you say?"

Emily almost said yes. She wanted to say yes, even though she also wanted to say no. Her head spun. Then the thought, unbidden, came to her mind: *you're not smart enough to do anything but take your clothes off.*

She winced inwardly. Plenty of women posed for photos and were also very intelligent, but Emily had a feeling she wasn't one of them. The thought was so depressing that she didn't answer Landon for a long moment.

"Well," he said, impatient. "Is that a yes?"

"I need to think about it."

"What's there to think about? This is a huge opportunity, Em. Huge."

"I know. And I appreciate you thinking of me. Really. But I need to think about it." She said the words more firmly now.

Landon sighed. "Fine. But I need your answer within the week. Otherwise I'm calling another one of my girls."

Emily walked home that afternoon with her mind in

turmoil. She'd gotten Josh out, yes, but she still needed money to pay the rent, to pay for groceries. To pay legal fees that Josh's arrest had incurred. The expenses continued to pile up, and Emily knew she'd be a fool to turn down Landon's offer.

Yet the thought of taking nude photos depressed her, because it proved what she'd always feared: she was a pretty face without a brain to match it. Only good to look at and nothing else.

Emily was looking forward to taking a nap, because God knew she was exhausted. Stepping inside her apartment, she heard music coming from Josh's room. When she saw his tennis shoes kicked off at the entrance, she stormed down the hall to his room.

"What the hell are you doing home?" Emily demanded as she swung open his door.

Josh started. He'd been lying on his bed, the music so loud that Emily had had to yell.

School didn't get out for another hour, and Emily knew for a fact that her brother didn't have a free period right now.

"Turn that down!" she shouted. When Josh didn't move, only scowled, she found the speaker and turned it off herself. "What are you doing home?"

Josh shrugged, as he always did. "I skipped."

"You skipped school," she repeated slowly.

"Yeah. Didn't you hear what I said?"

Emily swallowed down the anger that threatened to consume her. "Why?"

"Because it's stupid. What's the point? You never finished high school, so stop acting all high and mighty about it."

"I dropped out to help take care of *you*."

Josh flinched. "No one made you do that," he mumbled.

"No, no one made me. It was my decision, but I didn't have much of a choice to begin with. You're my brother, and when Mom died, I promised her I'd take care of you. I did my best, and for what?"

"If you're just going to yell at me, you're wasting your time. I'm dropping out and getting a job."

"So you've already made this decision without asking me?"

"I shouldn't have to ask you!" shouted Josh. "I'm not some little kid you can boss around anymore!"

"You're acting like a little kid right now."

"I'm dropping out because then I can get a job and I can help you." Josh turned pleading eyes to her. "I'm just trying to help, to make things better. Don't you get it?"

Emily crossed her arms, gripping her elbows until her fingers ached. She wanted to believe that Josh was sincere, but at this point, she couldn't. Maybe he would get a job, but then what? He'd have to work. He'd have to listen to his boss. He'd have to scrape together minimum wage just like she had to do, and she refused to let him throw his life away no matter how much he wanted to.

"You can't skip school," she said, "and you aren't dropping out. You're getting your high school diploma, even if I have to drag you to school every morning."

"Why the fuck do you care? The only reason we're broke is because you quit the one thing you were good at. You had money, Em! We had money when you modeled, but you couldn't hack it." Josh's lip curled. "So spare me your advice and your rules, because you don't know shit. We both know it."

Emily wondered if this was rock bottom, because she wanted to hurt her brother. His words pierced through her own rickety armor, drawing blood, and she wanted to draw blood from his skin, too. Only her barely maintained self-control kept her from lashing out like he'd just done.

"You're not skipping school again. That's final," she said.

"Whatever."

The anger that had been simmering boiled over inside her. A red haze covered her vision, as she looked at the brother she loved but at that moment couldn't like. The brother she almost wanted to hate and to abandon right then.

"Have you forgotten that you were recently *arrested*?" Emily took a deep breath. "You skipped school when you still have serious charges pending against you. When the judge is watching your every move. When skipping school could mean you getting remanded to adult court." With every word, her voice rose, until she was yelling, too.

"Are you fucking serious, Josh? Are you *fucking serious*?"

Emily rarely swore, and Josh's eyes widened at her words. But she wasn't done. That self-control? It dissolved. The only thing she felt right then was rage, and it overtook her mind, body, and soul.

"I've tried to be patient, Josh. God knows you've been through hell. I tried to be supportive and understanding and to let you figure things out." Her voice rose with each word. "But enough is enough. I've done everything I could for you, and you don't even have the basic decency to show that you're grateful. To care that I raised ten thousand dollars to get you out. So you repay me by skipping school?"

"I never asked you to do that!" he yelled. "I never asked you to get that money, and you know it. Don't blame me for that!"

"I am going to blame you for that, because what else could

I have done? Do you think I would've left you to rot in there? To get into more fights? Do you think that badly of me now?"

"Why does this have to be about you? I don't want you doing anything for me!" Josh got up, his fists clenched, his voice louder than she'd ever heard it. "I don't want you to be in my life if you're just going to control me!"

Emily stared up at him, at the little brother who was not so little anymore. "All I've tried to do is help you and love you," she said quietly. "If you see that as controlling, that's your problem."

"You'll never get it. You never have. You don't want to get it!" Josh picked up a nearby mug, dirty from coffee, and threw it against the wall in a violent motion. It shattered, the pieces of ceramic pinging to the floor.

Emily stared at the broken mug; then she stared at her brother. His face was red and he was gasping for breath.

"Get out of my apartment," she said. "If you're going to throw things at me? Get out. I don't want you here."

Josh bit back a sob, swiping at his eyes, but then he turned and grabbed his backpack. "Fuck you!" he yelled as he stormed out. "You'll never see me again if that's what you want!"

When the front door slammed closed, shaking the apartment walls, Emily closed her eyes and sank down onto the floor. She didn't cry. She was too wrung out to cry.

She began to collect the pieces of the mug, placing them on top of a towel that had been left on Josh's floor. When she picked up a large piece, she didn't realize that one side was as sharp as a thorn. It cut her thumb with ease. She hissed in a pained breath as blood welled behind her thumb's knuckle.

Strangely, Emily didn't feel the pain so much as the blood oozed down her thumb.

A memory came to her: when Josh had been all of six years old, he'd broken a glass in the kitchen. He'd been terrified that their mother would be angry with him, and he'd tried to clean up the bits of glass himself. When Emily had found him, he'd cut himself on one of the pieces. She found him crying, blood on the kitchen floor.

She'd cleaned up his finger and bandaged it. *I won't tell Mom*, she'd promised him. *It'll be our little secret. I'll tell her you cut yourself playing at school.*

The memory pierced through Emily's haze. A sob burst forth, and then another. Staggering to the bathroom, she wrapped up her thumb in toilet paper as the tears came in a torrent that wouldn't stop. She sat down on the toilet and sobbed until she was certain her heart was broken.

Emily didn't eat dinner that night. She waited for Josh to come home, praying that he would, and hating that she'd deactivated his phone months ago. She had no way to reach him. But where would he go? He couldn't stay out forever. His so-called friends had deserted him when he'd gotten arrested, and he had no money, either.

She waited up all night. When Josh didn't return in the morning, she told herself he would be home by the time she got off work. He had to come home. He just had to.

The first day, she told herself not to panic. The second day, she kept trying to tell herself not to panic.

But by the third day, she was in full panic mode, because her brother was missing and she knew it was all her fault.

CHAPTER TWELVE

Phin collected his things, exhaustion making him dream of going home and sleeping for the entire weekend. The court case involving a hit-and-run accident hadn't gone as well as he'd hoped, and now Phin was going to have to deal with the repercussions of his client being a no-show today at court.

Today was a day where Phin wondered why he did this job. What was the point when his clients refused to listen to his advice? When the outcome was that his client went to jail anyway? It was a pessimistic thought that he tried not to entertain for too long, but today it stuck in his craw.

Phin walked to his car with heavy steps. When he heard a voice say his name, he grimaced. He did not have the patience to deal with Sterling McIntosh today of all days.

"What a coincidence," said Sterling. "Seeing you here again."

Phin tossed his briefcase into the passenger seat of his car. "We're both lawyers. Not sure it's a coincidence so much as an inevitability."

"This is why you don't have any friends, because you

always have to correct people." Sterling said the words like a joke, but Phin knew the man wasn't actually joking.

"Did you need something?" said Phin.

Sterling's lip curled. "Can't an old colleague want to catch up without you suspecting some ulterior motive?"

"No, because you aren't just some old colleague. Stop playing coy, McIntosh. I'm not the mood."

Sterling shrugged. "Fine. I just think it's funny how high and mighty you are in the instep when we both know you're walking on glass right now."

"What are you talking about?" Phin said the words casually, even as his pulse picked up hearing the underlying threat.

"I've waited a long time, Younger, and I'll keep waiting until you fuck up. And I've heard you've been sniffing around a client a little too closely. You were seen with her out in public, embracing." Sterling smiled widely. "Isn't that against your code of conduct?"

Phin wanted to demand to know who had told Sterling about Emily, and who'd seen them. Had Sterling had someone following them? The thought turned his stomach.

"You're going to be waiting a long time," said Phin calmly, "because unlike you, I don't sexually harass the women around me." *I only kiss the ones who want me to kiss them…*

Sterling bristled. "You're full of shit and always have been. You concocted those charges against me because you were afraid of me—"

Phin snorted. "I saw you. In action, groping that poor girl." He shook his head as he opened his car door. "I don't have time for this."

"If you think I'll let this go, you're wrong. You better

watch your step, because I'll be there the second you screw up."

Sterling flipped him the bird and sauntered off. Phin briefly considered running Sterling over with his car. The only reason he didn't was because he'd rather not damage his relatively new car.

Phin had no idea if Sterling was just bluffing, or if he really had had someone who was feeding him information. Knowing Sterling, it could be a mixture of both. Wishing Sterling to hell and back again, Phin knew that he couldn't let himself fall further under Emily's spell.

Dating a client wasn't kosher, but it wasn't illegal, either. But if Sterling put up enough of a stink about it, it could hurt Phin's reputation and potentially jeopardize Josh's case. It didn't help that Sterling was the new DA and had the power to screw Phin over if he wanted to—and obviously, he wanted to.

When the two of them had been in law school together, Sterling had earned a reputation for being a schmuck. That hadn't surprised Phin, as Sterling had boasted about his sexual conquests around the other male law students as often as possible. There'd been rumors that Sterling had harassed multiple female law students, but there hadn't been any concrete proof.

Until the day that Phin had walked into a classroom and had found Sterling and a brand-new law student, Melissa, in what looked like an embrace. But Phin had soon realized this was no lover's embrace: Sterling had Melissa cornered, and when Phin had seen the terrified expression on her face, he'd grabbed Sterling and thrown him off her.

Melissa had run before either man could say anything to

her. Sterling had made excuses, had said that she'd been playing hard to get. But Phin hadn't mistaken the fear in Melissa's eyes. When he'd talked to her later, she'd agreed to report Sterling if Phin backed her up.

Phin had reported Sterling the next day, and although Sterling hadn't been kicked out, he'd lost his scholarship and had barely graduated. And after that, Sterling had vowed revenge.

Phin didn't regret reporting Sterling; he only wished Sterling's father wasn't a major donor to the law school. He'd essentially threatened to withhold his annual donation unless Sterling was allowed to stay in the program.

Some of the male students had sided with Sterling, while some had agreed with Phin. It hadn't been the best way to make friends, but Phin hadn't gone only to rub elbows with rich kids. He'd gone to earn his law degree and get to work.

"I can't see Emily again outside of the office," he said to himself when he arrived home. Not just for his career, but for her brother's sake, too. He had to defeat this simmering desire for her, this need to be her protector. He couldn't be that man, no matter how much he wanted to.

Phin had just finished eating his order of pad Thai when his phone rang. He didn't recognize the number, but that rarely stopped him from answering considering his profession.

"Hello?"

"Phin? Thank God, you picked up!"

Phin sat up. "Emily? What—"

"You have to help me." Her voice was frantic, panic-stricken. "I can't find Josh. He's gone."

"What do you mean, gone?"

She choked back what sounded like a sob. "We fought. I

said some things to him… oh God, I told him to get out, and he left. But he's been gone for three days, and I've contacted everyone I can think of, but it's like he's disappeared."

Phin grabbed his keys. "I'll come to your place. I'll be there in twenty minutes."

All of Phin's promises to himself that he'd stay away from Emily flew out the window the second he'd heard the desperation in her voice. By the time he arrived at her apartment, she was so frazzled that Phin could barely get her to explain the specifics of what had happened.

"Thank God you're here," she kept saying over and over again. "I didn't know what to do. I know I should call the police, but that'll get reported to the judge, and if they know he's run away—"

Emily covered her face with her hands. Phin gently peeled them away and led her to the worn couch in the living room. He went to the kitchen and got her a glass of water, making her drink it all.

"Take a deep breath. Another one. Panicking won't help us." Phin took her hands and rubbed them. "Tell me what happened, from the beginning."

Emily told him of the fight, how angry she'd been with her brother by the time he'd stormed out. She told him about how she'd deactivated Josh's phone months ago, so she couldn't reach him that way. She'd assumed that Josh would come back after a day or two, but now it had been three days with no word from him.

"What if he got into more trouble? Or he's hurt somewhere? He doesn't have any money, and I know his friends are worthless. What if he gets arrested again—"

"Stop." Phin tilted her chin up so she met his gaze. "You

can't do this to yourself. More than likely, he's with people he knows. Your brother seems resourceful, if a complete pain in the ass."

Emily's smile was wobbly. "I was so angry," she whispered. "I'd never spoken to him like that. I'm the one who's supposed to take care of him, and I keep failing."

"He's also not a child anymore. He's capable of making his own decisions, and he seems to be making them on his own no matter what you do." Phin's tone was gentle. "You can't destroy yourself over him. I've seen it too many times already."

Phin thought of his mother. Beatrice had loved her husband despite the abuse he'd inflicted upon her. She'd tried so hard to please him, even as she'd been plunged into her own mental illness. Their relationship had been completely self-destructive by the time Beatrice had taken her own life.

"We'll find your brother," promised Phin, knowing very well he shouldn't promise that, but he didn't care. "Let's make a list of the most likely places he'd be."

Emily finally calmed enough to start making a list while Phin asked more questions about Josh's friends and habits. Emily included places she'd already looked at the bottom of the list, chewing on her bottom lip as she considered anywhere else he might have gone.

"What about his friend, Reggie?" asked Phin. "He's still behind bars, but anyone connected to him?"

"I don't even know where Reggie lived." Emily sighed. "Josh kept all of that from me."

"Do you have Josh's phone still?"

"Oh, good thinking." Emily got up and returned with an

old flip-phone. "One of the perks of being poor is that I couldn't afford a smartphone for him. So no passcode."

They went through Josh's phone, calling and talking to everyone in his contacts list. Everyone who answered hadn't seen Josh at all. When Phin called Reggie's number, the line was disconnected. By the time they reached the last person on the list, Phin felt Emily's despair almost like it was his own.

"That rules out his friends," said Phin with a frown. "Then we'll have to do this the old-fashioned way: going out and looking for him."

It was already dark, and although Phin suggested that they wait until daylight, Emily couldn't wait. She grabbed a huge flashlight before she followed Phin to his car.

Although no one had admitted to seeing Josh, Emily still had Phin stop at one of Josh's friends' houses, one of the few whose address she knew.

The house in question was old and in disrepair, the windows covered in metal bars and a faded sign that said BEWARE OF DOG dangling from the chain-link fence encircling the property.

Phin knocked on the door, Emily behind him. Someone yelled inside, and then a woman opened the door a crack to say, "What do you want?"

"We're looking for my brother, Josh Lassiter." Emily got out her phone and showed the woman Josh's photo. "Have you seen him lately?"

The woman squinted at the photo. "I don't even know who that is. Nope, haven't seen him."

Before the woman could slam the door in their faces, though, Emily stepped forward and caught the door with her foot. "Josh is friends with Peyton, who lives here. Or used to live here. Do you know Peyton?"

The woman's face creased with suspicion. "Peyton's my son. Whaddya want with him?"

"We just want to talk to him," said Phin calmly. "Is he here?"

When the woman didn't reply, Phin said, "Josh has been missing. Any information would be helpful."

"Please," said Emily.

Finally, the woman relented and opened the door a little further. "Peyton!" she yelled up the dark stairs. "Somebody's here to talk to you!"

Peyton looked like he could be forty or fifteen depending on where you looked. He said nothing as he stood at the door, his mother next to him.

"I'm so sorry to bother you, but I'm looking for my brother." Emily once again showed the photo. "Have you seen him?"

Peyton scowled. "I haven't seen that shithead in months. Why you askin'?"

"Are you sure? He hasn't come by here in the last few days?" said Emily.

"I'm sure. He wouldn't dare."

"Is there anywhere you can think of that Josh would go?" said Phin.

Peyton shrugged. "Dunno. Like I said, I haven't seen him in forever."

Emily's shoulders sagged, and Phin wanted to put his arm around her. As if just noticing her, Peyton looked Emily up and down. "You don't look like Josh. You're his sister? You're way too hot to be his sister."

Before Peyton could say anything worse, his mother reached up and slapped him upside the head. "Don't be rude!" She shot Emily an apologetic look. "Sorry we couldn't help. Good luck."

Peyton rubbed the back of his head. "Geez, Ma. Seriously?" As he rubbed his head, though, he said, "I don't know where Josh is, but you might ask Mike."

Phin glanced at Emily. Mike hadn't been one of the people in Josh's phone.

"Do you have his number or his address?" said Emily.

"No, but Mike hangs out at the park down the street most nights." Peyton shrugged. "Mike ran away from home a year ago because his dad's a piece of shit, so that's where he lives."

It wasn't much information to go on, but it was better than nothing. Getting back into the car, Phin drove the few blocks to the park in question. Emily sat in the passenger seat, silent.

Phin prayed that this Mike person would have information, because if not, he wasn't sure where else to turn. If Josh stayed missing, Emily would need to file a missing person's report, no matter the consequences for Josh's pending charges.

Reaching over, Phin took her hand and squeezed it. She shot him a grateful smile.

"We'll find him," said Phin quietly. "Because if he misses his next court date, he'll have to deal with me."

Emily laughed. "That is a terrifying thought." She swallowed, her eyes shimmering. "I just hope he's safe, you know? I can't stand the thought that he's hurt somewhere, and that the last thing I said to him was that he should get out." Her voice wobbled now. "I'll never forgive myself if something happened to him and I never got a chance to apologize."

"Hey." They were near the park now, and Phin pulled over

and parked. "Hey, don't do this to yourself. You had every right to get angry with him."

"That doesn't mean I should've said those things to him."

"Maybe not, but you can't beat yourself up like this. We'll find your brother, and you can tell him yourself."

Emily choked back a sob. "Thank you. I didn't know who else to turn to, but I'm so glad you're here. I'm not sure I could've done this by myself."

Phin embraced her, despite the console separating them. Emily cried a little against his shoulder as Phin told himself that even though he needed to keep himself separate from Emily, he couldn't have told her no. What if she'd been wandering around this neighborhood by herself? The thought alone sent shudders through him.

"Come on," he said, wiping her tears. "Let's go find this Mike person, and hopefully your brother along with him."

CHAPTER THIRTEEN

Emily and Phin found Mike in the park as Peyton described, but to Emily's frustration, Mike was of no help whatsoever. He was drunk, or high, or both, and when Emily pressed him for information, he laughed and said she was wasting her time.

"He's a big kid," said Mike, his bloodshot eyes rolling his in head. "He'll come home. Or he won't. But you won't find him."

Phin looked like he wanted to take Mike and shake him until the few teeth remaining in his head fell out. Emily was tempted to do the same.

"Peyton said you might know where Josh is," said Emily.

Mike guffawed. "That stupid kid. Does he think I keep tabs on everyone this city? Jeezus, I can't even remember what I ate last."

"You don't have any idea where Josh might have gone? Nothing?"

"Lady, give it up." Mike gestured at Phin with his grizzled

chin. "Take your man home and cook him somethin' nice for making him come out here for no reason."

Emily opened her mouth to issue a sharp retort, until she felt Phin's hand on her arm.

"Come on," he said quietly. "We're wasting our time here."

Emily wanted to protest. She wanted to scream at Mike until he revealed something about her brother's whereabouts. How could he act like it wasn't a big deal? How could the world keep turning, acting like nothing had happened when Emily's world was falling apart?

She let Phin lead her back to his car, but when he told her he was taking her home, she balked.

"We can't stop now! We have to keep looking. We haven't even tried all of the addresses—"

"It's three in the morning," said Phin quietly. His gaze was tired, but steady. "We can try again when it's light out, but I'm not taking you around to every park in Portland at night. It's not safe."

"It's safe if you're with me."

Phin smiled grimly. "True, but I'm not taking you anywhere else. You're exhausted. When's the last time you slept?"

Emily hadn't slept in three days, and when she glanced in the overhead mirror, she saw a woman with dark circles under her eyes, her hair a mess. She hadn't showered; she'd barely eaten. She'd been so preoccupied with looking for Josh that she'd neglected herself.

"I'm taking you home." Phin started the car, and Emily found herself too tired to protest anymore.

When Phin got out of the car to follow Emily up to her

apartment, she expected him to drop her off at her door. Suddenly, the thought of going into her apartment alone was too much to bear. She didn't want to be alone tonight, and her exhausted mind wanted Phin to stay with her.

She shouldn't prey on his kind heart, but at that moment, she didn't care. Before she unlocked the door, she said, "Do you want to come in?"

Phin stared at her. She had a feeling that the answer to this question was bigger than even she understood. She waited with bated breath, praying that he said yes, and wondering how she would survive if he didn't.

"Okay," said Phin.

Emily's heart thrilled. She almost didn't care that her apartment was a mess at the moment because Phin was here, and he was standing in her living room, and he was strong and brave and kind. She'd never met a kinder man. As she slipped off her shoes, she took in the strong lines of his shoulders, how his hair just brushed his shirt collar.

"Do you want some tea?" she said. She needed to do something, something tactile; otherwise she was liable to throw herself into Phin's arms like a crazy woman.

Don't get your hopes up, Emily. He hasn't tried to kiss you since that one time.

After his affirmative reply, she bustled into her tiny kitchen. Setting the kettle to boil, she surreptitiously washed two mugs, making sure that one of them wasn't chipped.

She handed Phin the chip-less mug, steam rising lazily from the black tea, and she couldn't help but think of the mug Josh had broken before he'd stormed out. If she'd just kept her temper, if she hadn't gotten so angry at him…

But a part of her remained angry with her brother. What

she'd said to him had been harsh, but it had been honest. In a way, it had been freeing, although the results hadn't been what she'd wanted, either.

"Thank you," said Phin quietly. He sipped the tea as Emily considered whether she should sit on the couch next to him or on the chair opposite.

Feeling awkward, she chose the chair. Curling her feet under her, she drank her cup of tea, trying not to stare at Phin but failing miserably.

Was he horrified by her tiny apartment? He said he wasn't rich, but he was still a lawyer. He probably didn't have an apartment that smelled of old cigarette smoke, or have neighbors that screamed at each other every night. The carpet was patchy and burnt from the previous tenant, while the walls were yellow with age. Emily breathed a sigh of relief that her place no longer had cockroaches after a lengthy battle with the evil things.

"Thank you for your help tonight," she said, setting her mug down on the rickety side table. "I don't think I can ever repay you for it."

"You don't have to repay me. I'm glad you called me."

Her heart warmed at those words. Phin's eyes turned dark, and she wished she'd sat on the couch next to him. Her exhaustion seemed to melt away under that stare of his.

Her emotions were raw enough that she could admit how much she wanted him. She wanted to feel his arms around her, feel his mouth on her own. She wanted him to make her forget—and to convince her that within this world that seemed dark and hopeless, there was good and light, too.

"You're not like anyone I've ever met," she said, meaning it. "You don't expect anything in return. It's…refreshing."

Phin's lips quirked. "I'm not sure I'm that selfless."

"I think you are." She rose and sat down next to him. "I think you're amazing. You're smart, and funny, and you help so many people—"

He held up a hand. "I'm not a saint, Emily." His voice had turned to a growl that made her pulse pick up. "Believe me. The last thing I'm going to earn lately is sainthood. Don't put me on a pedestal."

"What do you want me to do, then?"

His gaze roved over her face, hungry, full of longing. She'd never seen such naked need on a man's face before. She'd seen lust, of course. Plenty of men had coveted her body, her beauty. But no one had looked at her and just wanted *her*.

"I don't want you to do a damn thing. I want you to tell me to leave, and I will."

Emily could barely breathe. "Why should I do that?" she whispered.

"Because it would be better than what I want to do. It would be better for everyone. For you, especially."

"I'm not going to do that."

He groaned, pushing his fingers through his hair. "You're going to kill me, aren't you? That's why you landed in my life. You're here to make me rethink everything, to doubt everything I've told myself."

Emily had no idea what he was talking about anymore, but all she could think about was that he wasn't leaving. She moved until their knees touched. She reached out and cupped his cheek.

"Stay with me tonight." She felt the stubble of his beard against her palm, a reminder of how human he was. "Because you're the first person who makes me feel like I'm not alone."

Phin groaned. He took her hand from his cheek and then kissed the center of her palm. Emily felt that kiss to her very center. She quivered, waiting, as Phin kissed her wrist, finding the pounding pulse there. His lips skimmed down her forearm, and when she felt the tip of his tongue taste the tendon in her arm, she bit her lip to stifle a moan.

"You're an addiction I can't defeat." He kissed her wrist one last time. He sounded like he didn't care that he'd been defeated. "I want you more than I've wanted any other woman."

Emily inhaled a shaky breath. She could feel how hard her nipples had gotten from that simple touch. "Then have me," she said.

One moment passed. Then another. And then Phin hauled her into his arms and kissed her like a man possessed, like he'd needed to kiss her for ages. She sighed and wrapped herself around him. Being in his arms simply felt right.

He kissed her until her bones melted. She ran her hands through his hair, the strands silky. This close, she could see how they glinted in the low light. His beard scratched at her chin as he kissed her, heightening the sensations.

"God," he said as he kissed down her throat. He licked at the pulse point in her neck. "What are you doing to me?"

He sounded like he truly didn't understand, and if Emily could've spoken, she would've agreed. But Phin's hands were relentless, skating down her body, cupping a breast while the other hand pushed her shirt up and touched the bare skin of her lower back.

Emily shivered. She could feel his hardness against her bottom, and she wiggled against him. He muttered under his breath.

"I've dreamed about this," she admitted. She touched his chest, felt his pounding heart under her fingertips. "Ever since that night that you kissed me. I thought you'd never do it again."

He smiled, although it wasn't a happy smile. "I told myself I wouldn't touch you again. But apparently I have no self-control where you're concerned."

Emily laughed, and then the laugh turned into a moan when he flicked her nipple through her shirt. She ground against his hardness, needing the friction, her body desperate for release.

She'd never been the type of woman to get hot and bothered by a few kisses and a boob grab. She could orgasm on her own without issue, but with a partner, it often took a long time or didn't happen at all. With Landon, he'd kiss her for a minute and then get bored. After a while, Emily didn't expect to come because she'd become convinced she wasn't worth the trouble.

Now, though, she had a feeling it hadn't been her, it had been her choice of lovers. She and Phin hadn't yet taken their clothes off, and Emily was about to burst.

Needing him to touch her everywhere, she pulled off her shirt. When she reached back to unhook her bra, he stopped her.

"Let me look at you," he rasped. His pupils were blown, a slight flush on his cheeks. He stared at her until she squirmed.

"Now you're making me nervous," she whispered. But then he leaned forward and kissed her over her heart before laving a path down to where the middle of her bra met her skin.

"You're so beautiful. The first time I saw you, I wanted

you." He pushed one bra strap down her shoulder and then the other. He looked up at her through heavy lids. "Let me see you, Emily. Because I've wanted to put my mouth on your breasts for weeks now."

She blushed even as she took off her bra, her breasts heavy and her nipples puckered. Phin made good on his word as he sucked one nipple into his mouth with a pressure that shot straight to her sex. She arched as he suckled and nipped, and she shivered when he blew cool air on the same nipple he'd sucked.

Emily rubbed against his cock, but Phin stilled her, his fingers digging into her waist.

"You're not going to come until I touch you myself," he murmured in her ear.

She was panting by the time he unzipped her jeans and delved inside her panties, and when his finger stroked through her wet folds, Emily whimpered.

"Goddamn." Phin kissed her neck as he played with her, spreading her moisture with his index finger. He circled her clit with light pressure—too light.

She didn't care that she was moaning and grinding against his hand. She was like a creature possessed with only one need, and she was so close already.

"So pretty. I wish I could see how pretty and pink you are, but I'm impatient. I want to see you come against my fingers."

Emily dug her nails into his shoulders as he pushed a finger inside her while his thumb rubbed her clit. She jerked, writhing, and it only took a few more strokes of his fingers to set her off. He caught her cry with his mouth. She sobbed, barely able to catch her breath, her orgasm ripping through her.

Emily kissed Phin, wordlessly grateful, her heart pounding in her ears. She began to unzip his jeans like he'd done for her. She molded her hand against his hardened length as he sucked in a breath.

She almost didn't hear the front door being unlocked. It was Phin who heard it first and pushed her away from him as he zipped up his jeans and tossed her her t-shirt. Emily stared at him, utterly confused, when the sound registered in her mushy brain.

Someone was here. Who would be coming into her apartment—?

She put her shirt on a second before Josh came into the living room. He looked pale, haggard, but when he saw Phin, he said, "What the hell?"

"Josh! Oh my God!"

Emily launched herself at her little brother, joy filling her as she realized he was home and he was okay. She hugged him hard, tears springing to her eyes.

"Where were you?" she demanded. "I was so worried! How could you run off like that? I thought the worst, that you were dead in a ditch somewhere—"

"Why is he here?" was Josh's reply, looking over at Phin.

Emily swallowed, trying to calm the blush spreading over her cheeks. She couldn't tell her brother about her relationship —whatever it was—with his court-appointed lawyer.

"Josh," said Phin as he rose, all professionalism now. "I'm glad you've returned home."

"You still haven't told me why you're here," said Josh.

"I was helping your sister look for you. We'd just been out searching for you." Phin's eyes narrowed. "She was worried sick."

Josh had the decency to look abashed, at least. "I'm sorry," he said to Emily. "I should've called."

"If you ever do that again, I'll send you to military school." Emily turned to Phin. "I'll walk you out. Josh, go to your room and we'll talk in a second."

Josh glared at Phin, and Emily had a feeling he knew that Phin hadn't just been here to help her search for him. How embarrassing!

Emily followed Phin to his car, wanting to say something, anything, but she was out of words for tonight. Her brain simply couldn't put together any coherent sentences.

"I'm glad Josh came home," said Phin.

He wouldn't look at her now as he stared off into the distance. Emily realized that he was already distancing himself from what had happened in her living room. Would he push her away like he always did?

"Phin, about tonight—"

Phin shot her an emotionless look. "It won't happen again. I promise."

A lump formed in her throat. *But I want it to happen again.* Old insecurities rose again, and she couldn't stop the evil little voice whispering in her ear that Phin wasn't any different from the other men she'd dated, who'd only wanted her body and nothing else.

They said their goodbyes. Emily watched Phin drive away, her heart hurting, not understanding why Phin kept helping her and then pushing her away from him.

CHAPTER FOURTEEN

August passed into September before Phin realized it, and as the leaves began to change, he became swamped under a load of work. He was grateful for it, because it gave him a reason to stop thinking about Emily. Each day he awoke, he considered calling her to tell her—what? That he was sorry? That he missed her?

He didn't call her, though. Josh's case was still pending, and there was nothing to discuss until his next court date, which was months away. As far as Phin had heard, Josh had been attending school and hadn't run away again. For that, he was thankful, because Emily didn't need the stress.

But Emily wasn't his to worry about. He'd made that abundantly clear when he'd touched her and then driven off. He hated himself for that. Yet when Sterling continued to sniff around him, he knew he'd made the right choice.

Emily didn't need Phin making her life harder than it already was. Logically, he knew that. In this instance, though, logic didn't soothe him like it normally would.

Tired to the bone, Phin arrived home late in the evening

in late September, bleary-eyed and wanting nothing more than to drink a beer and fall asleep on the couch.

His phone rang and interrupted his vegetative state. Normally he would ignore the call, but when he saw that it was Ash, he knew he couldn't ignore his brother.

"Yes?" answered Phin as he flipped through TV channels without really caring what he watched.

"You sound so happy to talk to me," joked Ash. "What are you doing?"

"Talking to you, obviously."

Ash snorted. "I've been meaning to reach you, because in case you didn't know, you never RSVP'd to my wedding, ya know."

Phin groaned. Shit, he'd forgotten completely. Not that he needed to officially RSVP, considering he was in the wedding, but Violet would want to know if he was bringing anyone.

"If you aren't coming, then you've wasted way too much money on a tux, little brother."

"Of course I'm coming," said Phin tiredly.

Phin heard Ash call, "Hey, Vi, he's coming! I told you!" Then to Phin, "Mostly I wanted to ask if you're bringing a date. I mean, we knew the answer was probably no, but Violet thought you should at least confirm."

"Violet is a kind person."

Ash chuckled. "She is, and she knows it. So just you, then?"

Phin was about to say yes when he hesitated. It wasn't that he cared what his family thought; they knew he was a loner. He didn't really even date. But right then, he didn't want to show up to his brother's wedding by himself. He didn't want to be Phin the loner, Phin the black sheep, Phin the workaholic lawyer.

"No, I have a date," he said before he could rethink his words.

Silence. Then: "Seriously?"

"You don't have to sound that surprised."

"Sorry. But I am. Surprised, that is. Who is she?"

Because apparently Phin was off his rocker, he answered, "Her name is Emily."

Ash was silent, like he hadn't expected Phin to have a name attached to this mysterious woman. Phin gritted his teeth in irritation.

"Why is that so surprising?" countered Phin.

"Hey, I didn't mean to piss you off. But you know as well as I do that you've never brought a woman to any family get-together. I think you even told me that it wasn't worth the effort because we were, and I quote, 'nosy and ridiculous.'"

Skewered by my own words. "You guys are all nosy and ridiculous."

Ash snorted. "Maybe Trent is. And Thea, to a certain extent. I don't ask awkward questions."

Phin couldn't help but laugh at that assertion. "Whatever you say."

"God, you're annoying. Why are little brothers so annoying?"

"Siblings in general are annoying."

Ash grunted. "I am happy to hear that you're bringing someone. Now that I have Violet, I realized just how depressing it is to be alone. I thought that it didn't matter, because I didn't need anyone else in my life. But I was wrong."

Phin was tempted to tell his brother to shut his mouth, but

Ash's words resonated inside him anyway. Phin had been lonely, but he'd pushed the feeling aside. It was easier to avoid entanglements. He'd told himself it was because he wasn't good with women, but had it been just an excuse? Now that he had met Emily, he had a feeling he'd been lying to himself for ages.

"How did you get Violet to forgive you? After you broke up?" said Phin.

"What did you do?"

"And you say you're not nosy."

"Touché." Ash sighed. "Ah, well, groveling is your best bet when you fuck up. Get-on-your-knees type of groveling. Because ninety-nine percent of the time, she's right and you're wrong, and you're just going to have to accept that."

"And if she doesn't forgive me?" asked Phin quietly.

"Then I guess you have to decide if it's worth the effort to keep trying to earn her forgiveness, or if you should let her go."

After the call ended, Phin put his head in his hands, wanting to laugh at himself. Why had he said Emily's name to begin with? There was no way she'd agree to be his plus one, even if he asked her.

Which he couldn't … could he?

"She'll probably tell me to go to hell," he muttered to himself.

Phin was never the type of person to be impulsive—that was Ash's purview. Where Phin thought and plotted and mulled things over, Ash tended to go with his gut and hope for the best. Phin had no idea what had gotten into him. How would he get out of this mess?

There was no way he'd tell Ash he'd lied. Best-case

scenario was that he showed up at the wedding without Emily, making up some lie that she couldn't attend. That made him wince. His family would never say so to his face, but they'd look at each other and think silently, *Poor Phin. Can't even get a date to his brother's wedding.*

He drank another beer, then another, thinking of a plan that would result in the least amount of awkwardness and humiliation.

Maybe he could apologize to Emily and just ask her. It was a risk, to say the least, but the thought of seeing her again was enough to get him to take the plunge. And as his date, she didn't have to act like they were actually together. They could simply attend the wedding together.

He snorted under his breath. Like he could keep his hands off Emily. His only hope was that Emily would tell him off and throw his offer in his face.

Ash had said Phin needed to grovel. Phin had never groveled in his life, but then again, he'd never met someone he'd wanted as desperately as he wanted Emily. He'd tried to forget her; he'd tried to move on this past month. It hadn't made a difference. No matter how many hours he worked, no matter how he focused on other things, he thought of her and he dreamed of her. She haunted him like some beautiful spirit.

He didn't know if Emily would forgive him for his hot-and-cold behavior toward her. But if he could get her to say yes… that thought alone sent a frisson of excitement through him.

His stupid, treacherous heart lifted, and he knew he couldn't go on without finding out what her answer would be.

～

JOSH HAD REFUSED to tell Emily where he'd gone the three days he'd been away, but since his return, they'd managed to agree on a tentative truce. Josh went to school—and stayed there—and Emily didn't ask too many prying questions.

As long as he wasn't skipping and wasn't hanging out with his former friends, Emily was satisfied.

She wished, though, that she could get Josh to open up, as she knew he was unhappy. She saw it in the lines of strain on his young face, the way he got up in the middle of the night to sit in the living room because he couldn't sleep.

She wished she could talk to Phin about her brother, but Phin hadn't spoken to her since that memorable night. He'd kissed her and touched her and had helped her to look for her brother and then—nothing. Except for the one email from him, which was all business, she might have wondered if he'd fallen off the face of the earth.

Emily tried not to feel hurt, but she failed. She wanted to demand answers; she wanted to know if her feelings had been one-sided. Yet the thought of getting an answer that told her point-blank that Phin didn't want her, had never really wanted her at all, would be too terrible to bear.

So she focused on working and on her brother, because thinking about Phin simply hurt too much.

That evening after her shift at the diner, Emily studied for her GED while Josh hung out in his room. He only came out for dinner and to use the bathroom most nights.

Emily slowly read through the passage from *Jane Eyre*, her brain tripping over the longer words. She powered through the passage until she reached the end and answered the question at the bottom. But Emily had been so focused on reading the individual words that she hadn't really paid attention to the story itself.

She had no idea what Jane's reaction was to Mr. Rochester in this passage. *If he's anything like most men, Jane was probably pissed and confused like all of us women are with men,* thought Emily acidly.

She worked on GED questions until her stomach rumbled. It was already past eight o'clock. Josh must be hungry, too.

"Josh, do you want pizza or enchiladas for dinner?" she asked through his door.

"Don't care," he said, which was usually his answer.

Emily sighed. She decided she'd bake the frozen pizza she'd bought earlier that week. Emily didn't mind cooking, but she rarely had time these days. Sometimes she brought home food from the diner, but most often she bought whatever was on sale at the grocery store. Frozen dinners crammed the freezer while their fridge tended to have only condiments, milk, and maybe a loaf of bread.

She'd be receiving her first royalty check from Landon soon. She just hoped he hadn't overstated how much those photos had earned her.

Someone knocked on the front door, but Emily ignored it. It was probably either a woman trying to sell cosmetics or a kid trying to raise money for his school. Emily didn't have any money to spare for either.

The person knocked a second time. "Emily, if you're in there, I want to talk."

Emily stared at the door, frozen in shock. Phin—he was here. Why was he here?

The sound of the oven timer beeping broke through her reverie, but she was so distracted that she almost dropped the pizza on the kitchen floor. Josh had emerged from his room, probably after smelling the pizza baking.

"Emily," said Phin through the door. "Please. We need to talk."

Josh frowned. "What the hell?"

"Josh, go to your room. I'll handle this."

Josh, because he never listened to her, just crossed his arms and stood behind her as she opened the door. And there was Phin, his reddish-blond hair falling into his eyes, his expression hopeful but strained.

"Dude, why do you keep coming to our house?" said Josh.

"Josh, please." Emily shot her brother an imploring look. "I need to talk to Mr. Younger."

Josh looked at her, then at Phin. His lip curled. He puffed out his chest as he said to Phin, "Don't do anything you'll regret."

Josh went to his room, but not before grabbing almost half the pizza. When he shut his bedroom door, Emily let out a sigh of relief.

Phin's hands were in his pockets, and he wasn't wearing his usual suit and button-up shirt. It made him seem more approachable, more human.

Emily was tempted to throw herself into his arms right then. But she held back. She leaned against the door frame and said, "Why are you here?"

He smiled grimly, like he wasn't surprised that she hadn't invited him inside. "Would you believe me if I said I was sorry?"

Oh, her heart fluttered at those words. "You came all the way here just to apologize?"

"Yes. I should've been straight with you."

"It would've made more sense than kissing me and then acting like I didn't exist." She didn't hide the hurt in her voice.

He winced. "I know. I just—you're a complication in my life."

"Is this supposed to be an apology?"

"Let me finish. I told myself I'd leave you alone, because there are rules for my work. I don't get involved with clients, and the last thing I wanted was to jeopardize your brother's case."

"Why didn't you just tell me that in the first place?"

"Because I'm an idiot." His smile was wry. "I thought I could forget you, but I was wrong." He reached out, like he was going to touch her, but then he dropped his hand. "You're an obsession I don't want to get over, Emily."

She closed her eyes. She should send him away because of all the reasons he'd just stated and then some. They were too different; they were from separate worlds. She thought of her GED study guide on the table inside. But right then, she didn't care about their differences. She only cared that he had come to her apartment to apologize and had told her the truth.

"So, what now?" she said.

"I don't know, but I'd like to do this for real."

She wanted to say yes so badly it was on the tip of her tongue, but she said instead, "What about all those things you just mentioned? I don't want to hurt your job. We can wait—"

"I don't want to wait. Dating a client isn't illegal." Phin's expression turned dark. "And I'll deal with anyone who tries to stop me."

She swallowed. "So, Phin Younger," she said, "are you asking me out?"

The smile he shot her made her insides quiver. "I guess I am. How about it? You want to go steady?"

She giggled, and then he had her in his arms. He hesitated, so she kissed him. They both groaned.

Being in his arms, feeling his lips against her own—both had never felt so right.

After they'd kissed long enough that they were panting, Phin said, "I'm also here to ask you to be my plus one for my brother's wedding."

Emily blinked. "You don't waste time, do you?"

"Will you go with me? Be my date?" He touched her cheek.

"Are you sure?" Because taking her to her brother's wedding was basically a declaration to the world that they were together.

"I'm sure."

Emily's heart almost burst right then. Oh God, she'd already fallen for this man, hadn't she?

"Okay," she said. "I'll be your date."

CHAPTER FIFTEEN

Since Phin was a groomsman in his brother's wedding, he needed to be there a few days beforehand, so Emily told him that she'd take the train up to Seattle the morning of the wedding. Phin had balked at first, but after she'd agreed to let him pick her up at the train station, plans had settled into place.

"I talked to Violet, and she said you could hang out with her and the rest of the wedding party at her house," said Phin as he pulled up at a charming bungalow house in north Seattle.

Emily's heart pounded with nerves. She would be introduced to the entirety of Phin's family. Would they like her? She couldn't bear to think that they'd dislike her.

"I'll take you inside and introduce you." Phin took her hand and squeezed it. "They'll love you, I promise."

Phin opened the front door without knocking, calling out, "Violet? Thea?"

A woman with short blond hair and a septum ring came skipping down the stairs. "Phin! Finally!" The woman hugged

Phin hard before turning to Emily. "You must be Emily. I still can't believe Phin brought somebody. The last time he brought anyone home, he was in fifth grade, and we teased him so mercilessly that he never did it again. Maybe that's why he's so stand-offish."

"*Thea…*" hissed Phin.

Emily bit her lip to stifle a laugh. "It's nice to meet you. You're Phin's sister Thea?"

Thea beamed. "He mentioned me? That's a shock." She slapped Phin on the shoulder. "This little brother of mine is the worst, you know. I hope you're giving him hell. He never comes home, never calls, never makes sure his dear old sister is even still alive—"

"Don't you have Anthony for that now?" said Phin wryly.

Thea shrugged. "You're still my brother." Thea then took Emily's arm to lead her upstairs. "Phin, get out of here. This is a ladies-only zone. Go to Trent's to get ready and get drunk."

"No one is getting drunk!" a voice yelled from the top of the stairs. Emily smiled as she recognized Violet, who was hiding behind a wall, only her head and neck currently visible. "Sorry, Phin," she said, "but I'm not dressed. Go make sure Ash behaves himself, please?"

Phin saluted. "I'm on it." Then he turned to Emily, saying quietly as he touched her cheek, "I'll see you later, okay? Text me if you need anything."

After Phin left, Emily found Thea staring up at her in amazement. "He must really like you."

Emily blushed. "How can you tell?"

"He brought you here, didn't he? And he touched you in front of other people?" Thea tapped her chin. "You know, I wasn't sure what you'd be like, despite Violet saying you were cool. My baby brother is a special dude."

"I know."

"Good, because even though I'm shorter than you, I'll beat you up if you hurt him." Thea smiled so brightly that Emily could only laugh at the supposed threat.

Upstairs, Emily met Phin and Thea's youngest sister, Lucy, who was a gorgeous blond with an irrepressible energy and a sweet laugh. She also met Lizzie Younger, née Thornton, who was Trent Younger's wife. A toddler sat on the floor in front of her, playing with toy horses, and based on the size of Lizzie's belly, a second child would be along soon. Emily couldn't help but envy how much Lizzie glowed with her pregnancy.

The last woman Emily met was Violet's older sister Vera, who was the oldest of the bunch but joined in the conversation without missing a beat. She and Violet didn't look much alike, but Emily could see a resemblance in their smiles.

"Emily, right? Sit next to me. I want to hear all about how you met Phin," said Lizzie.

The toddler looked up at Emily with wary eyes. "Who are you?" she asked suspiciously.

"This is Emily, Uncle Phin's girlfriend. Emily, this is my daughter Bea."

"It's nice to meet you, Bea," said Emily seriously. The little girl looked just like her mother, although their eye colors were different.

Bea considered this before saying, "Is Uncle Phin getting married?"

Although it took Emily a second to understand what Bea was saying—toddler speak wasn't Emily's forte—she blushed bright red when she realized what the question was.

Thea burst out laughing. "Bea, you're worse than me. Come on, let's play so you don't make her start crying from embarrassment."

Bea was soon distracted by her aunt's antics, which Lucy joined in a few moments later.

Emily couldn't stop herself from imagining a wedding where she was the bride and Phin the groom. It was a ridiculous fantasy—but then again, hadn't Phin wanted to make this real? Wasn't she his girlfriend now? Her heart stuck in her throat at the very thought of becoming Phin's wife.

"Sorry about that," said Lizzie. "She takes after her father."

"Lizzie, don't lie. You want to know all the details like we all do," said Thea.

Lizzie bit her lip. "It's true, but if you don't want to talk about it—"

"No, I mean, there isn't much to tell." Emily recited the story, leaving out the worst bits of Josh's charges, making it sound like a very normal way to meet and start dating.

Lizzie studied her, much like Bea had done earlier. "I don't know Phin super well, but he's always seemed…"

"Aloof?" supplied Violet, who was doing her makeup at the moment.

"You guys are terrible," said Vera with a laugh. "Didn't you say you'd leave Emily alone? I swear you all promised that right before she got here."

Thea shrugged. "I never promised that."

"Phin is the definition of aloof," said Lucy, completing Violet's sentence. "He's always been like that. Even as a kid he would always do his own thing."

"The fact that he pursued you at all says a lot." Lizzie's

voice was quiet but sincere. "I'm so glad he's found somebody. I always sensed that he was lonely, although he'd never admit it."

Emily's heart squeezed. Part of her still didn't believe she was good enough for Phin, but she hoped she was nonetheless. She hoped that what his family said was true, too.

"Dammit." Violet tossed an eyeliner pencil onto the table with a deep sigh. "Why did I say I'd do my own makeup? I should've hired a professional." She turned to the group. "Can anyone do a cat-eye?"

"Only if I mess up five times beforehand," was Lucy's reply. Thea just laughed, and Lizzie put up her hands in defeat.

Emily, though, got up and picked up the pencil that Violet had tossed down. "I can do it," she said.

"You can? Oh, that would be amazing. I can usually do a decent job, but I'm so nervous that I can't keep my hand steady."

"I used to do my own makeup for shows. We had a makeup artist on the bigger ones, but sometimes a girl has to make do," said Emily.

"That's right, you were a model, weren't you?" Lucy came to sit nearby. "I want to hear all about that. I've considered doing some modeling."

"Lucy wants to be a famous actress," explained Thea.

Lucy blushed a little. "I just want to be an actress who can pay her bills."

"I know about that all too well." Emily touched Violet's chin to turn her face toward her. "No, keep your eyes open. It'll be easier since you have hooded eyes."

"Is that why my eyeliner is always wonky?"

"Probably. I have hooded eyes, too. Make things tricky, but not impossible."

Emily concentrated on doing Violet's eyeliner, going into the zone she'd enter when she used to model. The conversation around her seemed to quiet to a murmur, and within a few minutes, she'd given Violet a perfectly sharp cat-eye.

"I love it! This is perfect. Thank you!" Impulsively, Violet hugged Emily.

Emily felt a rise of emotion in her chest. She hadn't had female friends in a long time, not with working and trying to keep Josh out of trouble. The few model friends she'd had had drifted away after Emily had quit the business.

But Emily was soon distracted by the rest of the group asking for her to do their makeup, and by the time they were all getting dressed for photos, Emily felt like she'd made friends out of these women she hadn't even known hours earlier.

As PHIN WALKED down the aisle at Violet and Ash's wedding, wearing a tuxedo and hearing the violin and cello play behind him, he couldn't help but wonder what his own wedding would be like.

He'd never in his life thought about such a thing, because he'd always assumed it wasn't something that would happen. Yet as he turned to face the guests, he sought out Emily in the crowd.

She was easy to spot—in the second row in the bride's section—and she smiled at him as their gazes caught. She wore a blue dress, her hair in a simple top-knot. Phin's heart pounded seeing her like this. It was almost unbearable that he couldn't go to her right then, that he couldn't sweep her up in his arms and kiss her and tell her how beautiful she was.

He could do that soon, he told himself. He forced his attention on the ceremony. When Violet came down the aisle on her father's arm, everyone seemed to sigh collectively. Ash stood proudly, and Phin smiled when he saw his older brother dash a tear from his eye as Violet joined him at the front.

But Phin's eyes were for Emily. As Ash and Violet exchanged vows, he imagined doing the same with Emily. Normally, that kind of thought would've terrified him, but now? Now it only energized him.

He wanted what Ash had. He'd told himself he didn't need that—a wife, a family, a home together—but he'd been wrong. He'd been lying to himself for years.

When Ash and Violet kissed, now husband and wife, the guests and wedding party erupted into cheers. The kiss went on so long that Violet finally pushed Ash away with a breathless laugh, and somebody wolf-whistled in the crowd.

Phin shot Emily a smile as he walked behind the wedded couple, mouthing, *I'll see you soon.*

Phin was happy that Ash and Violet had done photos before the ceremony, because that meant everyone could attend the reception immediately. The sun had just started to set as the guests walked down a short path; the reception would be held in a huge pavilion, Lake Union shimmering right below.

It felt like days before the usual reception activities ended and the dancing began. Phin rose and went to Emily's table before anyone could snag his attention.

He might be here for his brother, but he couldn't help but feel like he was truly here for Emily.

"Dance with me?" he said.

Emily smiled and took his hand. "I didn't think you danced."

"I don't. But it's the only way I can get you to myself right now."

She shivered, especially as his hand moved to the bare skin between her shoulders. Her dress was simple, a blue V-neck gown that emphasized her neck and collarbone, with just a hint of cleavage. Three-inch nude pumps made her tall enough to reach Phin's shoulder, while delicate silver-and-crystal earrings jingled softly as she moved.

"You look beautiful," said Phin as the music began. "I'm sorry I left you today. I was almost tempted to tell Ash that I wasn't going to be a groomsman."

Emily laughed. "I wouldn't have let you do that. Besides, I had a lovely time with the girls."

At Phin's arched eyebrow, she added, "No, really. Your sisters are very sweet, and your sisters-in-law, too. Even your niece. It's kind of ridiculous."

"My siblings are a pain in the ass." But as he said the words, he couldn't help but smile. "I'm glad you liked them, though."

They danced, the rest of the wedding guests falling away, and Phin drank in Emily's smile, her soft laugh as he attempted to twirl her around. He couldn't help but think of how she'd moaned his name as he'd touched her that night in her living room.

As if reading his mind, color rose in her cheeks, her eyes

turning glassy. He had the sudden desperate need to kiss her again. He dipped his head down to say, "Come with me."

She nodded dazedly as he led her outside the pavilion. The moon was heavy and bright overhead, providing them with just enough light as they wandered into a garden nearby.

Pushing Emily against a vine-covered wall, Phin gathered her into his arms and kissed her. She responded instantly, touching his hair, her tongue darting into his mouth with an ardor matched only by his own. He groaned her name as he kissed her. He couldn't just kiss her—he needed more. He needed her under him, crying his name. His cock was so hard that it was painful.

Emily pressed needy hands against his shoulders. When he rubbed his hardness against her belly, she inhaled sharply.

"I want you," he said, guttural, never having felt this desperate for a woman before. "Come to my room?"

"What about the reception?"

"I don't give a flying fuck about it right now. I want you under me. I want to be inside you, and to hear my name on your lips as I make you come."

She quivered at the heated words. He kissed down her throat, inhaling the sweet scent of her perfume. Her skin was warm and soft as silk, and he wanted to touch her everywhere.

"Say yes. Say yes, Emily."

She licked her lips, a movement that shot straight to his groin. "If no one will notice us being gone—"

"I don't care if they do."

She brought his head down so she could whisper into his ear, "Then yes. Make me yours, Phin."

CHAPTER SIXTEEN

Emily followed Phin into the nearby hotel, saying a silent prayer of thanks that Ash and Violet had thought to have everything for the wedding within close proximity.

Phin headed straight to the elevator, and when the doors closed with only the two of them inside, he started kissing her again. She'd never kissed a man in an elevator. But then again, she hadn't been this desperate to be with a man in her entire life. All of her previous relationships paled in comparison to this lust burning through her.

Phin nipped at her bottom lip before kissing the side of her mouth. "That beauty mark has driven me crazy since I first saw you," he admitted. "It made me want to kiss you right then."

"In the courtroom? That judge would've had quite a show."

Phin laughed. "Honestly, it probably wouldn't have been the craziest thing he's seen. It would've probably been a regular morning for him."

At that, Emily started laughing, and she almost demanded

to hear some of Phin's crazier stories. But then the elevator stopped, and Phin's gaze turned serious as they stepped into the deserted hallway.

"That day I first saw you," he said quietly, "I wanted to take you away from everything. Keep you safe, locked in a tower, away from anything and everyone who could hurt you."

Her eyes widened.

"But I never thought you'd let me." His mouth twisted. Before Emily could ask him why, his mouth took hers, and they stumbled to his room between kisses.

Phin finally got the door unlocked with some swearing. Then he pushed her against the wall, his hands all over her, taking over her every sense. She could only taste, touch, see Phin. She didn't want it to be any other way.

Both of them panting, Emily began to untie his bow tie with shaking fingers. "I love you in a tux," she said, her heart slamming against her ribs as she revealed his golden skin under his shirt. Leaning forward, she licked the spot at the base of his throat. He groaned and cupped the back of her head.

Emily wasn't a stranger to men desiring her. They'd always desired her body, and when she'd been younger, she'd believed that they could love the rest of her, too. But as Phin watched her, his eyes luminous, she could see something in their depths that told her no man had looked at her like he did right this moment, like she was a goddess he'd never expected to find.

She unbuttoned his shirt before pushing up his undershirt until she could touch warm, bare skin. He grunted as she kissed the hard wall of muscle that was his abdomen, and she raked her fingers through the crisp hair on his chest. When she tried to pull his shirt all the way off, he laughed in a low voice.

"Cufflinks," he said, raising his arm to unhook them.

Emily hadn't known that watching a man unhook cufflinks to reveal his forearms could be so erotic. She felt her body respond, as if he had his hands on her again, and when he was finally bare-chested, she could've melted at his feet.

"You're beautiful," she marveled. She kissed his heart, pounding against his sternum.

"I don't think that's an adjective anyone has used to describe me."

"No?" She smiled as she began to unbuckle his belt. "How about smart, funny, handsome—"

"Emily," he growled.

"Oh, and definitely big, hard, and impressive." She cupped his hardness through his slacks. "Yes, definitely impressive."

"Christ." He pushed her hands away and turned her around. He unzipped her dress, the hiss of the zipper a counterpoint to the sounds of their panting. When he kissed the nape of her neck, she arched back toward him.

"This dress. I never thought a dress could make me this crazy."

She laughed, a little uncertain. "It was twenty dollars, too."

"The best twenty dollars ever spent in the history of the universe."

Her dress soon puddled at her feet, and she was clad in only her thong and strapless bra. She tried to turn around to face Phin again, but he kept her against the wall. He palmed her ass.

"You're like some kind of fantasy, Emily. Jesus, this ass." He dipped his finger into the triangle of her thong before pushing it to the side. His clever fingers soon touched her where she needed him most, and he groaned when he found the wetness there. Her sex throbbed with need, even as he spread her wetness through her folds, teasing her until she wanted to sob.

Emily was already on the edge. But then Phin knelt and pushed her legs apart until he could put his mouth on her core, licking wetly, she struggled to keep standing. Her knees were water, her spine jelly.

"God, you're amazing." He groaned, kissing her, his tongue making her see stars behind her eyelids. She cried out when he sucked her clit before pinching it. Pleasure and pain mixed together in a heady whirl. Only a few more strokes of his clever tongue and she came, her body shaking so hard that it was only Phin's arm around her waist that kept her from falling to the floor.

He caught her mouth, and Emily could taste herself on his tongue. It only aroused her more. She needed more—she needed him.

"I need you," she said. "I want you inside me."

Phin kissed her hard at the admission, and it was only a few moments later that they were on the bed. Phin had shed his slacks and briefs. Emily's breath caught as she gazed upon him: his cock hard and ruddy, his cheeks slightly flushed, his reddish-gold hair brushing his forehead. Sweat gleamed on his chest, and Emily couldn't stop herself from licking a drop from the same place at the base of his throat she'd kissed earlier.

"I'll be right back. Don't move," he said in a voice that brooked no argument.

Not that Emily would move. That first orgasm had just been a taste, an appetizer, and she needed more. She needed all of this man.

Phin returned with a bunch of foil packets, a wry smile on his face. "My brother," he said with a light laugh, "made sure that the hotel supplied the rooms with plenty of condoms."

"Seriously?"

"Seriously."

Phin ripped open one of the packets, but Emily plucked it from his fingers.

"Your brother is a smart man." She slowly unrolled the latex down Phin's cock, and she could've sworn it grew larger under her fingers.

"Smart, and fucking annoying."

"I wonder who else is going to hook up at this wedding?"

Phin growled. "Christ, I don't care. I only care about being inside you and making you come on my cock."

Emily shivered, her heart pounding so hard she could hear it in her ears. She kissed Phin as he pushed her onto her back, her legs widening of their own accord. She lifted her pelvis, and when his cock brushed against her sensitive clit, they both let out noises that sounded like something out of a wild animal.

Phin held her hips and pushed inside her, slowly, inexorably, his cock so thick that Emily had the brief fear that he couldn't fit. But then he was kissing her as he simply let her adjust to his size, and in that moment, she knew she'd given him her heart already. She'd thought that she could sleep with him without getting attached. She'd been wrong—so wrong.

Especially when he began to move, his thrusts touching not just a spot inside her that drove her out of her mind, but a part of her heart that she'd thought dead. She gasped and writhed, she clawed at his shoulders, and she kissed him as he pounded harder into her.

"Phin, Phin, Phin," she said in a litany.

"Fuck, Emily—"

She could've laughed at the normally austere Phin turning into a man of many words, but at that moment, she didn't care. She just wanted this to never end.

Her belly tightened, and when Phin reached down to rub her clit, she detonated. He caught her scream in a kiss as she shook so hard that the bed shook with her. Her own orgasm seemed to create a chain reaction. Before long, Phin let out a shout and came, too, his cock flexing inside her.

A few deep breaths later, Phin rolled away from her, taking her with him. Emily felt dizzy. Could you faint from amazing sex? She bit back a hysterical laugh at the ridiculous thought.

The sex was amazing, but the way Phin gazed at her and took care of her afterward was what broke her heart. After he'd disposed of the condom, he brought a washcloth and touched her with it so gently that she almost cried. After he'd wiped himself down, he tossed the washcloth into the bathroom and returned to the bed.

Her heart in her throat, her emotions going every which way, she clung to his arm like a lifesaver in the sea and just hoped that she could hang on for the journey.

PHIN CONSIDERED sex an inevitable necessity to life. Like

eating, or sleeping, or going to the dentist every year. Although sex was more enjoyable than going to the dentist by far, Phin had never had any sex that he could've described beyond enjoyable.

Phin lay awake, Emily passed out next to him, and he realized that he'd been wrong. Completely, utterly wrong. Sex with Emily had destroyed everything he'd thought was true and had set him completely adrift. It was like he'd thought he would just remodel a single room and had returned home to find his house reduced to complete rubble.

What did you do when your own heart was the rubble in question?

He reached over and touched Emily's hair, which had fallen out of its updo hours ago. It was currently fanned across both her pillow and his, and he smiled like a man obsessed. He kissed her cheek, smiling wider as she snuggled further into sleep, snoring softly.

He'd never watched a woman sleep. His previous lovers had never stayed the night, because they'd never wanted to. They'd wanted sex, he'd wanted sex, and that was that. But now Phin could sit here all night, gazing at Emily as she slept, without a care in the world.

The sheet had slipped down, exposing the bare line of Emily's smooth back. Phin danced his fingers down her spine, marveling at how silky-soft her skin was. He licked at a mole near her shoulder blade.

She shivered as he reached the dip of her lower back and kissed the top of her ass, which was shaped just like a heart.

"What time is it?" she said softly as she came awake.

He hadn't meant to wake her, but he couldn't regret it. "Late. Early. Depending on how you look at it."

She laughed. "Helpful." She turned over, which gave him a full view of her luscious breasts. Tipped with dark brown nipples, they were high and small, but shaped perfectly. Everything about her was perfect.

If he thought too hard about what she saw in him—who was hardly anything perfect—he'd start to go down a vicious road of self-doubt and recriminations. But the darkness of the room, the smell of sex and Emily's perfume, and his own desperate need for her were enough to distract him from his own overly busy mind.

He licked at one nipple, rolling the bud around his tongue. Emily inhaled sharply. Her belly turned concave, and Phin danced his fingers down her torso until he could reach the promise land between her thighs.

She was already slick, but as he rubbed her sex and kissed her breasts, her wetness increased until they were both shaking.

"Phin." She touched his hair even as her hips bucked against his touch.

He brought his fingers to his mouth, sucking each one in turn. Emily's eyes widened, but he could also hear her breathing increase. He didn't think he'd ever get enough of her taste, of her reaction. Of the tight grip of her sheath around his cock as she came.

Emily sat up, and to his amusement, she pushed him onto the bed so she could climb on top of him. She grabbed a condom from the bedside table, and after she'd sheathed him in the latex, she slowly sat herself upon his length.

His eyes rolled back in his head at her heat clenched around him. Emily rocked slowly, her hands on his shoulders, her head tipped back with her hair almost touching her ass.

"So fucking beautiful." Phin twisted her hand around his fingers, tugging gently, and her hips picked up speed.

Their gazes locked as she rode him, faster and faster, and it took all of Phin's self-control not to explode before she did. His balls drew up against his body as her sheath began to tighten around his cock.

"I'm coming, oh my God—" Her voice was lost in a cry as she shook.

Phin exploded as he emptied himself inside her. Drawing her down, he kissed her as they both shook from the conflagration that had gripped them so tightly.

Phin barely remembered getting rid of this condom and getting back into bed. When he drew an arm around Emily, her head on his shoulder, it was only a second later that his eyes closed and he fell into the dreamless sleep of the satisfied and sated.

CHAPTER SEVENTEEN

Emily awoke to the smell of coffee and the sound of rustling paper. She groaned before she stretched her aching muscles, blushing bright red when she remembered the cause of those body aches. Who also happened to be sitting next to her in bed, watching her nude stretching without batting an eyelash.

"Good morning," rumbled Phin, a smile on his face. "There's coffee. I thought we could order room service if you're hungry."

Emily needed a shower and, based on how fuzzy her teeth were, a toothbrush. "I need to go to my room and get my suitcase."

"I got it for you." At her surprised look, he pointed to the bag in the corner. "I got your room key from your purse. I probably should've asked, but—"

"Oh, no. Thank you. I think I'll go take a shower."

"I'll order us some food, then."

As Emily stood under the hot water of her shower, she couldn't help but wonder at this feeling in her belly. She felt...

unsettled. Her fuzzy mind came to the conclusion that it wasn't that she was unhappy about sleeping with Phin, but that the fact that he wanted to take care of her was something she knew would take time to get used to.

Emily had always been the one to take care of people. She couldn't remember the last time she'd relied on someone else. When was the last time someone had made sure she had clothes and food? Not since her mother had died. She'd been the one to worry about such things ever since then.

Emily combed her wet hair in thoughtful silence. She heard the door open and close, and her stomach rumbled when she smelled food. She hadn't realized it until that second, but she was starving. She hadn't eaten since yesterday afternoon, before the wedding. She'd been too distracted by Phin to eat at the reception.

Donning a robe, Emily found Phin at the table, food covering the surface. She marveled at the variety: fluffy eggs, bacon, fruit, waffles, scones.

"Are other people joining us?" she asked in surprise.

"No, but I didn't know what you liked, so I just ordered every breakfast available. Although if there's something else you'd like instead, I'm sure we can get it."

Emily sat down, her heart in her throat. She piled her plate with food, trying not to sneak glances at Phin and failing miserably.

He must've shaven while she'd been asleep, because the stubbly jaw she'd felt against her skin last night was gone. She shivered at the memory. Last night had been explosive. Unbelievable. Had it really happened?

Phin's eyes heated, as if he could read her thoughts. He bit into a piece of bacon and chewed thoughtfully.

"This is really good. Thank you for getting food," said Emily. "Although I'm not sure how we'll eat all of it."

"I think I could eat all of it myself, given last night's activities." Phin drank his coffee, as casual as could be.

Emily snorted. "You're such a guy."

"I'm glad you've noticed," he drawled.

She stuck out her tongue, which made him laugh. Soon, the initial awkwardness of waking up in the morning with someone faded. They chatted about the wedding, Emily wondering if anyone had noticed their absence. Phin just shrugged at the question.

"If anyone did notice," he said prosaically, "I don't care."

Emily couldn't help but agree with that sentiment.

After breakfast, they lounged in bed, neither of them needing to drive back to Portland anytime soon. Yawning, Emily snuggled against Phin and considered going back to sleep. But the thought of returning home made her wonder if this would last much longer.

Phin might've asked her to be his girlfriend, but she didn't know what would happen once they returned to reality. Her own insecurities nipped at her, making her doubt how much he wanted this to be a real relationship.

"You seem contemplative this morning," he said quietly.

"I'm always contemplative after multiple orgasms," she quipped, not wanting him to sense her morose thoughts.

He grinned. "Multiple? I think there were at least five—"

"Now you're just making things up—"

"No, I counted." He leaned down and whispered in her ear, "First, when I licked you until you came, the second…"

He proceeded to list each one, and Emily wanted to jump

his bones by the time he got to orgasm number four. She needed to add six and seven to the list, pronto.

But right then, Phin's phone rang, and when he saw the number, he grimaced. "Sorry, I have to take this. Do you mind?"

Emily sighed and shook her head.

She listened to Phin talk lawyer speak, her mind drifting as she barely listened to the conversation. It wasn't like she could really understand what Phin was talking about, anyway. It was like listening to someone speak French—complete nonsense to her ears.

"Can you get my briefcase?" whispered Phin to Emily. "It's on the desk."

Emily returned with his briefcase, handing it to him, but he put up a hand. She was now rather tempted to pinch him. She wasn't his secretary!

Phin began to riffle through the briefcase before pulling out a blue folder. But as Emily shifted in the bed, she bumped into him and he dropped the folder, sending the papers inside drifting around them both.

"Shit—no, sorry, not you. I dropped the folder."

When Emily began to collect the papers without his asking, he mouthed *thank you* and she shot him a wry smile. One document had somehow gotten under the bed, and she had to wiggle under the frame a bit to snatch it.

"Which form? The one for the Smith case?" Phin glanced at Emily. *Can you get that for me?* he mouthed before he turned away to scribble notes on the notepad on the nightstand.

Emily froze, heart in her throat. There were at least thirty pieces of paper in her hand, all of which were filled with legal jargon and paragraphs filled with words that she couldn't begin to read. She began to flip through the pile, hoping that some word would jump out at her. But as her gaze scanned each page, the words began to twist, the letters flipping around.

"No, we're looking for it right now. We? Oh, my secretary," lied Phin with an apologetic look at Emily. *Do you have it?* he mouthed.

She shook her head. She wasn't going to find it. Should she pick a random one and hope it was the one he wanted, or should she lie? She decided lying would be better, even though she hated deceiving Phin.

"I don't see it," she said, hoping he didn't notice the wobble in her voice. "Sorry."

Phin frowned. "Hey, I'll have to call you back in a bit. Yeah, I know. You'll live." He hung up and took the pile of papers from Emily, sorting through them. "I didn't mean to get you involved, and this is definitely a violation of client-attorney privacy, so anything you read? Forget it."

Emily almost laughed hysterically. "It's already forgotten." She tapped her temple.

"Oh, here it is. It was the third paper in the bunch." He glanced at Emily, and her heart seized.

Does he know? Has he guessed my secret? She could hardly bear the thought. It was too humiliating.

He kept looking at her, like she was some mysterious being he'd never seen before.

"I should start packing," she said, apropos of nothing. "I have a train to catch this afternoon."

"I thought you'd be riding back with me." He sounded confused now.

Emily shook her head, not looking at Phin right then.

"You'll want to see your family. I don't mind riding the train. It's nice." She kept babbling, picking up various pieces of her clothing that had been scattered after last night, blushing at the memories they invoked.

She found her dress on the floor, grimacing at how it had been handled but also glad that she hadn't spent hundreds of dollars on it. She folded it and placed it inside the small bag that held a dingy makeup bag, her second change of clothes, and not much else.

"Emily," said Phin, and she could hear him approach her. He touched her shoulder. "What is it?"

"Nothing." Her voice was too cheery. She took a deep breath as she said more calmly, "Nothing. I just need to start packing."

"Emily." His tone was firmer.

Now she had to turn to look at him. Wishing she could melt into the floor, she waited for the axe to fall on her neck.

"Are you going to tell me what's wrong, or am I going to have to pry it out of you?"

PHIN HAD TRIED to sound like he was joking, but when Emily's eyes widened, he winced inwardly. So much for trying to put her at ease. But then again, he'd been right: something was wrong with her. What had caused the sudden shift in her behavior?

Did she regret their night together? That thought alone made his heart sink into his toes. She was acting cagey, like if he moved too quickly she'd strike at him. She wouldn't look him in the eye, either.

"Please don't make me talk about it," she whispered. "Please."

Paranoia snaked through him. *Oh God, she wants to end things. She wants to tell me it's over but doesn't have the heart to do it.*

His voice was raw as he said slowly, "I'd rather you be honest. Because there's no use acting like everything is fine if that's not the case. Believe me: I know when people are putting on a show."

Emily looked like she wanted to run out of the room. "I didn't mean to keep it from you," she said in a small voice. "I didn't think it would matter to you."

He stared at her. "It wouldn't matter to me? Of course it matters. Why would you think that?"

"I guess I thought you were a different kind of guy," she snapped.

Phin reeled back. Emily's face was stark white now, and Phin was afraid she might faint. Rather afraid she'd bolt or swoon, he made her sit down where they'd been happily eating breakfast only an hour earlier.

Emily kept tugging at her hair, her movements jerky, her expression anxious. She looked like she might throw up. Phin wanted to reach out to touch her, but he had a feeling she would reject him for it.

Didn't I tell myself relationships never worked for me? That they weren't for me? I messed this up before it even began.

"I knew this wouldn't work out. I knew I was just deluding myself," muttered Emily, as if Phin didn't exist anymore. "I told myself over and over that I should let you go, and I was right, but I hate that I was right—"

Phin interrupted her monologue. "Can you at least explain yourself? I don't think I understand anything right now."

"Why should I? You've already made up your mind about me. I'm a total idiot. I already know that! I'm not going to beg you to change your mind."

Maybe paranoia had been Phin's first feeling—now he was angry, frustrated. Rising from his chair, he said, "You don't have to keep insulting me. You clearly regret our night together and are doing everything in your power to get out of seeing me again." When Emily didn't reply, he knew he'd hit the nail on the head. "So why don't you just leave already and save us all the trouble?" he said quietly.

He wished she'd deny what he'd said. He wished she'd tell him that she didn't regret anything, that she wanted to make this work. But when she remained silent and pale, her expression both angry and aggrieved, he knew that wasn't going to happen.

"Then I think it's best that I leave." She gathered her things, her chin held high.

Phin wanted to go to her, but he just curled his fingers into a fist and did nothing.

He opened the door for her. "Then I guess this is goodbye."

"I guess it is. Goodbye."

Phin closed the door without a sound, but it was as deafening as a gunshot. He should be relieved that things had ended without a nasty battle. He knew that—but all he could feel was desolation that it was already over.

CHAPTER EIGHTEEN

Emily's stomach rumbled as she smelled the burger and fries waiting for her latest table. She hadn't eaten since early that morning, and the diner had been so busy that she'd only had time to eat a quick granola bar on her break. Normally she tried to avoid the greasy meals here, but right then, she could've eaten that entire plate and then some.

Jenson eyed her as she gazed longingly at the plate. "You hungry?" he grunted.

"No."

"Yeah, you are." Jenson pushed the burger and fries toward her. When she balked, he said, "I already made too many. Eat it. Otherwise I'll trash it."

Emily was skeptical this was the case, but she wasn't about to look a gift horse in the mouth. Taking the plate, she found her favorite corner in the kitchen and chowed down. She almost moaned with pleasure as she took her first bite. She ate the entire plate in record time, practically licking it when she was done.

"Thanks for that. I should get back to work."

Jenson didn't say anything; he didn't need to.

Emily knew that both Lawrence and Jenson were protective of all of their waitresses, but she'd always thought they looked out for her more than the others. It was probably because she didn't have anyone at home to look out for her. Josh was hardly a great candidate for that task.

Her smile wobbled as she thought about Phin, because any subject that could be remotely connected to him brought him back into her mind. It had been two weeks since she'd gone to his brother's wedding. She hadn't gotten a single text from him, not a phone call—nothing. She'd told herself it was for the best, because if he was horrified by her lack of reading ability (and a part of her hoped she was wrong about that), she shouldn't want anything to do with them.

And yet…her heart hoped she was wrong. She hoped that he hadn't texted because his phone had fallen into the Pacific Ocean. She hoped he was just too busy to call. She hoped, and she hoped some more, knowing full well that with every day that passed, her hope shrank until it wouldn't fill a thimble.

Emily was just thankful that Josh was still attending school and keeping out of trouble. That, at least, was one worry off her mind—for now. Who knew how long Josh's good behavior would last?

At the end of Emily's shift, she heard Lawrence call her name. He motioned at her to follow him to his tiny office in the back of the diner.

"Sit. How was your shift? You get good tips tonight?" said Lawrence.

Emily eyed him askance. "Did you ask me back here just to chat?"

"Maybe." Then Lawrence sighed, rubbing the back of his neck. "Jenson says you ate a burger tonight."

"I'm sorry, he said that he'd made extra. I should've asked you. I mean, I know we can order whatever we like, but it was a customer's order—"

"No, I don't care about that. What I mean to say is: do you need anything?"

Emily blushed to the roots of her hair when she realized what Lawrence was asking. "I'm fine. You don't have to worry about me."

"I wish I could believe you, but you've gotten thinner, Em. I know this place doesn't pay much, but I don't want to think about any of my employees going home hungry. If you needed help, you'd tell me, right?"

"Of course," she lied. She forced a smile onto her face. "Did you need anything else?"

Lawrence let her go without any more questions. She felt both touched and humiliated that her normally gruff boss had asked her the question at all. But she had stopped eating as much, now that Josh was back. She told herself she was too busy, but she knew that she didn't have the money to buy three square meals for both herself and her growing teenage brother.

At that moment, everything felt so heavy that Emily wanted to sit on the sidewalk outside the diner and just cry her eyes out. Why did she have to choose between things like food or rent? When would she see the light at the end of the tunnel?

"Em! I'm glad I caught you."

Emily stared in surprise as Landon approached her, a

cheery smile on his face. But when he caught her expression, his smile faded. "What's wrong?"

"Nothing." She wasn't about to tell Landon her troubles. "Why are you always stalking me outside my work?"

Landon's smile turned crooked. "Maybe I wanted to see you in person. You're a tricky person to track down, Emily Lassiter."

His voice was flirtatious, his eyes dancing, and Emily braced herself for the inevitable question that would follow.

"I need to get home. My brother will be wondering where I am."

"I doubt it. Isn't he fifteen now?"

"Sixteen."

"But if you're headed home, I'll walk you."

Emily couldn't find a reason to tell Landon no, so she just nodded. For a block, he didn't say anything, and she wondered what his game was. If he wanted to do another photoshoot with her, he would've told her already.

"You're probably wondering why I came by your work again," he said. He touched her arm, stopping her. "I've been thinking about you a lot lately. How we used to be, you know. We were good together, weren't we?"

Emily almost laughed. Landon had dumped her when she'd needed to focus on things like earning money to pay her rent. If that was "good" to him, she didn't want to know what he considered a bad relationship.

"Landon—"

"No, hear me out. I've missed you."

He smiled that sunny, surfer boy smile that had once made her heart pitter-patter. Now, it only annoyed her.

"I want you back," he added. He took a step toward her. "Can we try again?"

Emily thought of Phin. In comparison, Landon was like a golden retriever versus a wolf. She couldn't imagine going back to someone like Landon when she'd experienced pure ecstasy in Phin's arms, even if just for a night.

"I'm sorry," she said, almost meaning it, "but I can't."

"Can't? Or won't?"

"Does it matter?"

"Yeah, because I'd like to know the reason why." Landon's eyes flashed. "Is there someone else?"

Why was it that men would only leave a woman be if you told them you were another man's property? Irritation filling her, she snapped, "That's none of your business."

It was clearly the wrong thing to say, because Landon latched onto it like a dog with a bone. "Who is it?"

She started walking. "I don't want to talk about this."

"Well, tough shit. I do." Landon grabbed her arm—not enough to hurt, but enough to get her to stop again. "Who is it? Otherwise I'm gonna assume you're lying, and I hate liars."

"Do you really want me to tell you I'm just not interested? Fine, I'm not interested. We broke up, and I got over it. That's all there is to it."

Emily was about to walk away again when Landon said, "Is it the lawyer? The one your brother is using?"

She stopped, her heart in her throat. "How did you—?"

Landon's mouth twisted. "I have my ways. And you weren't being subtle about it."

"Then why ask me out in the first place?"

"I wanted confirmation. I didn't think you'd go for a suit

like that. Seriously? Somebody like that? So, are you together or not?"

"And I keep saying: it's none of your business."

Landon leaned against the brick wall behind him. "So that means he fucked you and ran." Landon sighed. "I could've told you that would've happened. A guy like him wants women who can keep up with him. Women who know what lawyers do, you know."

The voice in Emily's head that had made her walk out on Phin came roaring back to life at Landon's words. She knew she should walk away, but it was like she was rooted to the spot. Her limbs were frozen, and so was her tongue. She could only listen as her heart cracked.

"Did you tell him you can't read?" Landon's voice was sad, but mocking. "Did you tell him you're basically as smart as a fourth grader? Or did he fuck you first and then you told him and he got bored instantly?"

The frozen feeling in her limbs vanished. Red hot with rage, she slapped Landon across the face, so hard that her palm stung. He swore in outrage.

"What the fuck!" he yelled. He touched his bloody lip. "You fucking hit me!"

"If you think I'd ever get back with you now, you're insane. Go to hell, Landon. Don't ever speak to me again."

She was glad that Landon didn't come after her. Then again, he'd said what he'd wanted to say to her, hadn't he?

With every step, she felt his words push deeper into her heart, like dirty needles. She felt the infection spread, no matter how hard she tried to ward it off.

Her heart breaking, she stumbled into the apartment,

ignoring Josh asking her what was wrong as she went to her room, locked the door, and cried.

"Phin," said Linda, "can you come to my office?"

Phin was tempted to tell her he didn't have time, but the serious expression on his boss's face brooked no argument. By the time Phin was sitting in the chair across from Linda, he felt like her stare could see right through him.

"I got an interesting phone call today from the district attorney's office. Apparently, there's reason to believe that you've gotten involved with one of your clients here."

Phin's jaw clenched, knowing full well who the person was who had called. "If you mean that I'm dating my client, then no."

"You *were* dating her?"

"Yes, but it's over now."

Linda sighed, a deep full-body sigh as she leaned back into her chair. "Normally, I'd say watch yourself, or at the very least, you should've waited until the case was finished. You're not one of my employees who I have to worry about—usually. But this takes it to another level entirely." Linda's gaze was sharp. "Why would someone want to throw you under the bus, Phin?"

Phin was tempted to keep what had happened between him and Sterling a secret, but what did it matter? He hadn't done anything wrong. He recounted the story to Linda, and she remained silent even after he'd finished talking.

"I've never liked that slimy son of a bitch," she said finally, her lip curling. "Sterling tried to get a job here. Did you know that?"

"Really?"

"I didn't even let him interview." Linda smiled grimly. "I'd heard rumors about his behavior; I'm almost glad that they've been confirmed. That being said, you dating a client—whether it's over or not—has put you in the line of fire. Do you think anyone saw you with her?"

Phin didn't know. He hadn't been as discreet as he should've been. But when it came to Emily, it was like all of his hard-won common sense had gone straight out the window.

"I took Emily to my brother's wedding two weeks ago," he admitted.

"Shit, Phin. That's not just a fling—that's a declaration. This could be used against you to take you off this case, if you've overly influenced the client's sister. Did you sleep with her?"

Phin didn't respond to that question, because there was no reason to.

"Never mind. All we can do is deny and lie low. You said it's over between you? You won't make this worse by continuing to pursue her?"

"No. It's over. She already told me as much."

Linda let him go after that with a word of warning, but Phin was too enraged to care that his boss was now involved. Sterling had been watching him, just like he'd said he would. But Phin hadn't taken Sterling's threats seriously because Sterling had always been full of hot air. Then again, this was also the first time Phin had stepped out of line in his entire career.

Emily had somehow managed to upend his entire world within only a few weeks.

"What was that all about?" said Katherine as she came into Phin's office. "Linda looked pissed."

"If you can believe it," he said wryly, "I fucked up."

Katherine's eyes widened. "You? I can't believe it. You're the most boring person ever when it comes to the rules." Her eyes got wider. "Is it your client? Emily? Oh my God, tell me everything. Otherwise I'm going to make Linda tell me instead."

Phin gave Katherine the bare-bones story, not letting her ask questions during his recital. He wondered how many people he'd have to spill his guts to today. Would his entire family show up at his door tonight and demand answers? He wouldn't put it past the fickle ways of the universe right then.

"You took her to your brother's wedding?" Katherine was incredulous. "When I said you should date her, I thought…"

"What?"

"I guess I just didn't think you'd let yourself get close to her. You never do. You go through life on your own, Phin. But taking her to your brother's wedding, meeting your family? That's huge."

"You don't sound upset about it."

"Why should I be? I'm happy for you. This whole thing with Sterling will blow over." Katherine waved a hand. "You haven't done anything wrong. What can he do?"

Phin sighed. "A lot, if he pulls some strings. Don't be naive, Katherine."

"Maybe, but will he? He might just want to make you squirm without following through. I've always found that people are usually more prone to apathy than outright malice."

"I'm not sure how comforting that statement is."

She smiled. "Don't let Emily go. She obviously means a lot to you. Are you in love with her?"

Phin tried to hide his reaction to that question, but obviously he wasn't a good enough actor. Katherine inhaled sharply.

"Oh, Phin." Her voice turned gentle. "You need to get her back."

"How? When she told me point-blank I wasn't the man she wanted?" His voice was hoarse with pain.

"You said yourself she misunderstood that conversation you had. You need to explain, and you need to show her that you care."

"And then what? Tell her everything just so she can reject me again?"

"Maybe. Or maybe not. Maybe she's waiting for you as much as you're waiting for her. So who'll break the silence first? If you love her, or at least have strong feelings for her, then she must be worth the risk."

Phin rubbed his temples. "I've always felt like I wasn't meant for this kind of thing," he confessed. "I've never been good at relationships. Feelings. Making a woman care about me."

"Have you ever thought that maybe you need to put in effort to make that happen? That maybe women had been interested in you, but when you acted aloof and unavailable, they decided you could never want anything with them?"

It was ridiculous that Phin hadn't ever thought that, but it was like the clouds parted and the sun shone on him for the first time. Had he unconsciously pushed people away while telling himself people couldn't understand him? It made a twisted kind of sense.

"The funny thing about love is that you have to put your heart on the line to get it," said Katherine. She touched Phin on the arm. "It'll probably be the scariest thing you ever do. But it's worth it. I promise you."

CHAPTER NINETEEN

Saturday morning, Emily awoke to find Josh already up and making coffee. Considering her younger brother could barely make toast without burning it, she was shocked to find him making coffee in the first place.

"I didn't know you drank coffee," she said.

"I started drinking it when I was in juvie."

"It's early for you to be up." Normally Josh didn't get up until midday on weekends.

He shrugged. "Couldn't sleep."

Emily slumped down onto one of the rickety kitchen chairs. "I couldn't either. I kept staring up at the ceiling no matter how hard I tried to shut my eyes and sleep."

The coffee machine beeped, and Josh brought two mugs to the table. Emily stared at her brother in surprise. Where had the angry, selfish teenager gone? She kept getting whiplash from Josh's personality changes; she was half-certain she'd get a concussion soon enough.

"Did something happen last night?" said Josh. He was decidedly not looking at Emily when he asked the question.

Last night—Emily swallowed, her throat dry. She shouldn't have let Landon get to her like he had, but it had been like the straw that broke the camel's back. She was already hurting over Phin, and Landon had only added to that burden.

"I ran into Landon. You remember him?"

"Yeah." Josh's lip curled. "I never liked him."

"Really?"

"He always acted like he was better than us. He'd give me those stupid gifts and then act pissed when I didn't suck his dick in gratitude."

Emily winced, although she had to agree with Josh's assessment. "Well, he said some things to me that made me upset. That's all."

Josh stirred his coffee with a straw, but Emily could see the way his fingers clenched around the handle of the mug.

"What happened, Josh? When you ran away?"

Josh flinched. Emily had tried to get Josh to talk about what had happened, but he'd told her in no uncertain terms never to ask again.

"It doesn't matter," he said.

"Then why won't you tell me?" At his continued silence, she said softly, "Nothing you'll tell me will make me hate you or send you away again. I should never have done that. I can never apologize enough for doing that."

"It's nothing to do with that."

"Then what is it?"

Emily could see Josh's barriers breaking down, and with a mutter under his breath, he said, "I saw a guy overdose in the park. Is that what you wanted to know?"

"Oh, Josh. Tell me what happened." She took his hand

and squeezed it, and she was thankful that he didn't push her away.

"I was sleeping on a bench. There was lots of homeless people around, although they mostly left me alone."

"Were you scared?"

"Of the homeless people?" He raised his eyebrows. "No. Most of them were too strung out to give a shit about me. They wanted more drugs or booze, and I had no money to help them get it. One guy gave me half a sandwich when he saw me staring at him. That was the guy who died. I was starving and I sat down on that bench, and this guy sits down below a tree not far from where I was, unwrapping this sandwich. I was too out of it not to stare. He noticed, and when he got up, I thought he'd tell me to fuck off. But he didn't. He said nothing, just gave me half and sat back down."

Emily smiled sadly. "I'm glad he did that."

"I'm not, because I owed him for that and I couldn't do a damn thing to help him." Josh swallowed hard. "I fell asleep— I don't know what time it was. But I woke up to people talking. Somebody was yelling something. The guy who'd given me his sandwich, he was on the ground. A woman shook him, like he was just asleep.

"I shouldn't have gone to look, but I couldn't help it. His eyes were staring up at nothing. He was breathing, but barely."

"He was still alive?" Emily's heart clenched.

"Yeah, but not for much longer." Josh wiped his eyes roughly. "I asked everybody there if they had a phone to call 911. And every person told me that it was a waste of time. Finally, one guy told me to shut the fuck up because if the police came, it'd make trouble for everybody." Josh grimaced.

"I didn't even think about that. Then I remembered that if I got arrested, I'd be fucked, too.

"The woman who'd shaken the guy told me he'd taken so much heroin that nobody could survive it, that he'd wanted to die and had told her as much a week ago. A few minutes later, he stopped breathing. I watched him die, and I couldn't do anything. I was totally useless."

Emily was crying now. "Josh, I wish you would've told me."

"That I'm a fucking coward who couldn't do anything to help a dying man? I wasn't going to tell anybody that." Josh put his head in his hands. "He was nice to me, and what did I do? Nothing."

Josh made a sound of such pain that Emily wrapped her arms around him. He cried, finally, and she cried with him.

"I should've called an ambulance. Something. Somebody must've had a phone. I should've asked everyone in that fucking park."

"You did the best you could. You were the only one willing to call at all. That means something. I'm proud of you, Josh."

Josh let out a noise that sounded like a wounded animal. Emily just hugged him, wishing she could find the words to comfort him and knowing there were none.

"I keep having nightmares about what happened. That I'm that guy on the ground, dying, and nobody would do anything about it," said Josh.

"Is that why you've decided to behave yourself lately?"

He let out a bitter laugh. "Maybe. Scared the shit out of me."

"I'm not glad that that happened to you, but I'm glad that

you started to see sense." Taking a deep breath, Emily then said, "I hope this means you'll take the plea deal."

Josh's face closed, as it always did when they talked about this sore subject. "I already told you: I'm not ratting out my friend."

"How can Reggie be a friend when he's put you in this position? Think, Josh! I know you think this 'snitches get stitches' code is somehow brave, but it's not. It's stupid. Reggie doesn't deserve your loyalty, and he obviously doesn't care about being loyal to you."

Josh crossed his arms and refused to look at her now.

"That guy in the park who died," said Emily quietly, "what if he'd gotten a second chance? What if someone had given him a lifeline and he wouldn't have had to die like that? Because that's what this is for you. A lifeline. A second chance. You could serve only a little time in a juvenile detention center instead of prison. You could get out and have a real life and not be branded a felon. Because what happens when you get out of prison? You won't be able to get a job hardly anywhere. You won't be able to get a loan for a car, or go where you want to. It'll be a sentence that lasts your entire life.

"If you won't do it for yourself, then at least do it for me. I've already spent ten thousand dollars and counting on this. So you owe me, Josh. Do the right thing for once."

Josh didn't say anything for a long moment. Emily felt exhaustion sweep through her, and she considered going back to bed. If Josh wouldn't listen to her now, what was the point? She wasn't going to beg him to take the plea deal.

"Fine," he said roughly. "I'll do it."

Her heart soared. "You will? Oh, Josh—"

"Don't. Just, leave me alone, okay?"

He stormed off and slammed the door to his bedroom. Emily, though, didn't care how angry he was right now. She could only feel elation—an elation that made her want to tell someone about this.

Grabbing her purse, she yelled, "I'll be back later!" and headed out to see the one person who could share in the celebration.

DESPITE IT BEING SATURDAY, Phin still came into the office that morning. Going to Ash and Violet's wedding had put him behind on work. It didn't help that sitting at home by himself only intensified how much he missed Emily.

No one else was in the office, for which Phin was grateful. He didn't need a repeat of yesterday's drama. Despite Katherine's assertion that he should go after Emily, Phin wasn't entirely certain he should. Why press the issue when he already knew what she would say?

Or you're just a huge coward, his mind told him scathingly.

"I can't believe you're working today," said a voice in the doorway. And there was Emily, standing in his office, like he'd wished for her and she'd appeared.

He stared at her, incredulous, wondering why she looked so happy to see him at all.

"I'd forgotten it was Saturday right before I came here, and then I thought, 'he won't be here because it's the weekend.' But I saw your car, so I knew you were here."

"I don't understand," was all he could manage.

Emily blushed, realizing how crazy she sounded. "I wanted to tell you that Josh will take the plea deal." Her voice rose with excitement. "I finally got him to agree. He's not happy about it, and he probably will never forgive me, but he said he would. Isn't that wonderful? I'm so relieved. I knew I had to tell you right away."

Phin almost asked her why she couldn't have called or emailed or, hell, sent a carrier pigeon instead of showing up in his office like this. And why did she have to look so damn beautiful, wearing only jeans and a worn t-shirt, her hair in a messy bun?

"That's great news. I'm glad your brother realized that it's the best option for him. I'll start putting the paperwork together immediately."

Emily bit her lip, and the movement shot straight to Phin's groin. His blood heated; he gripped his pen so hard it almost snapped in two. God, he still wanted her, even after everything that had happened between them.

"You're doing well?" he said, because he couldn't think of anything else to say.

"Well enough, considering everything." She was shy as she asked, "And you?"

I've missed you like crazy. I don't care what you said back at the hotel. You could tell me to go to hell and I'd still want you.

"I have a lot of work to get done. I'll let you know when I have everything ready for your brother. I hope we can get a satisfactory conclusion to all of this."

Emily visibly deflated. "Oh. Okay. Thanks." She went to the door to leave, but then stopped. "I shouldn't have come here. It was stupid of me. I was so excited about Josh that I wasn't thinking. It won't happen again."

She had her hand on the door handle when Phin said, "Stop. Wait." He stood behind her, only a hairsbreadth from touching her, and he could see the goose bumps rise on the back of her neck from his nearness. "Why did you come?"

Emily didn't turn to look at him, but he could see her shoulders stiffen. "I told you. And I won't bother you again."

"You're not bothering me."

She whirled to face him. "Really? Then why do you act like I have the plague right now? Are you really that disgusted about what you realized back at the hotel?"

"What I realized? You mean you telling me that I wasn't the man for you?"

"I'm not talking about that." She drew in a deep breath. "I'm talking about my…learning disability. That I can't read. And you acted like I'd murdered your entire family." Her face was drawn, pale, her lower lip trembling. "And I was stupid enough to come here to see you! I should've learned my lesson. But I thought—"

Phin stared at her in utter confusion. "What the hell are you talking about? That you can't read?"

Emily blinked as redness rose in her cheeks. She whispered, "That morning in the hotel room…" She took a deep breath. "I thought you figured out my secret. That I can't read. That's why you sent me away."

Phin couldn't believe what he was hearing. He'd thought she'd decided he wasn't the man for her based on…what? His own issues? He didn't even know at this point. And she'd thought he'd rejected her because she couldn't read.

She couldn't read—she couldn't *read*! That was what she'd been hiding. It all made such perfect, ridiculous sense. If he could've dared to laugh, he would have.

Phin took her by the shoulders, searching her face, hope rising inside him. "Emily, I don't give a damn about whether you can read or not. Do you think I would think less of you because of something that's obviously not your fault?"

"But—"

Phin laughed bitterly. "I'm a lawyer, but apparently I have the comprehension of a gnat. I thought that you didn't want me, Emily. That's why I said those things that I said. If I'd known that you believed it was because what you told me…" He shook his head. "I'm an idiot. I'm so sorry. I hurt you, and there's no excuse for that. I should've run after you and explained myself, because I've been tying myself in knots over what happened."

"You really don't care that I can't read?" Her voice was small, and it broke Phin's heart.

"No." He tilted her chin up so she'd look at him. "You're amazing. Beautiful, kind-hearted. Resilient. Nothing you could tell me would make me think otherwise."

Her chin wobbled. "I'm so ashamed of it. I didn't want you to know because you're so smart. You have a law degree. I'm a high school dropout who can't even get her GED. I'm a nobody."

"You are the woman who stopped me in my tracks the second I first met you. The woman who fought for her brother, even when that brother didn't deserve it. The woman who's fought against adversity but never lost her sweetness and goodness, either." Phin pushed his fingers through his hair. "Christ, who am I to that? I've locked myself away from people my entire life. I have a career and nothing else." His lips twisted into a semblance of a smile. "At least people will remember you when you're gone."

"You don't give yourself enough credit."

When Emily placed her hand on Phin's chest, his heart

sped up. They gazed at each other, the moment lengthening, and Phin could feel desire pulse between them. It was like something alive, something with a heartbeat, and as he caressed her cheek, it was like the last puzzle piece of his life fell into place.

He kissed her, because he couldn't not kiss her. She moaned, wrapping her arms around him, and Phin picked her up and placed her on his desk. He pushed everything else on the desk onto the floor. The crashing sound made Emily giggle, but her giggle was swallowed as he kissed her.

"I've missed you," he said as he yanked her t-shirt over her head. Her plain white bra was the sexiest thing he'd ever seen in that moment. He palmed one breast as he sucked the other through the thin fabric.

Emily's head fell back as he touched her. She was soft as silk, smooth as water across a lake. He wanted to consume her and lock her away in a tower so that she'd be his for all of eternity.

"I want to see you," she whispered.

Emily unzipped his pants and palmed his cock; Phin groaned to the ceiling. When she squeezed him at the base, he almost came right then and there.

It only took a few more moments for Emily to get out of her jeans. Phin pushed her panties to the side and found her soaking, her wetness coating his fingers and palm as he played with her. She shivered when he brushed her clit with his thumb.

"I want to watch your face as you come," he said, his voice guttural. He stroked through her folds before circling her clit.

Her pupils were blown, her cheeks rosy, and as he rubbed her and dipped a finger inside her tightening sheath, he watched her. In one moment she was gasping, and in the next she screamed as she shook with her release. Phin kissed her hard, and she kissed him back, their tongues tangling.

He needed to be inside her, but he realized that he didn't have a condom. It wasn't like he kept a basket in his office. Groaning, he dropped his forehead on her shoulder.

"What is it?" she said.

"Condom. Do you have one?"

Emily stilled before brushing the nape of his neck with light fingers. "I'm on the Pill," she whispered. "And I'm clean."

"Are you sure?"

"If you think I'm letting you leave without finishing this, you're insane."

He chuckled. He grasped her hips, notching his cock against her slick opening, and then he slid inside her. His toes curled into his shoes from the feeling of her, bare and hot and slick. Her nails dug into his shoulders as he pulled out and thrust inside her to the hilt. The desk shook under them with every movement.

When she came a second time, it triggered his own orgasm. He groaned as he poured himself inside her. By the time he'd finished coming, he felt like he'd been wrung completely dry.

He didn't move for a long moment. Emily kissed his shoulder where her nails had bitten into his skin.

"That was…" said Phin after they'd both cleaned up and dressed.

"I love you," she admitted, not caring that they were in a parking lot, or that Phin had never intimated that he felt the same.

Phin stared down at her. He looked astonished, like he'd never seen her before. "Emily…"

"You don't have to say anything. I don't want you to if you don't mean it. I just wanted to let you know."

"Christ, Emily, I don't deserve something like that."

She smiled sadly. "Do any of us? That's why love is such a powerful thing, when it's given freely. And I do give it to you freely."

CHAPTER TWENTY

Once Josh decided to take the plea deal, things moved more quickly than Emily had expected. By the end of October, she was sitting in the same courtroom where Josh had been charged. Josh sat with both Phin and his JCC officer, Harry Benson, and he hadn't looked back at Emily once.

Emily blew out a breath. Her heart was still pounding hard, and she was glad she was behind the trio of men. Otherwise, she was afraid she might faint. Or sob. Or both.

When everything began, Josh finally looked over his shoulder at Emily. He shot her a wan smile. She prayed that the judge would accept the deal and be merciful toward Josh.

Phin had warned her that Josh could still spend time in a juvenile detention center. She hated the very thought, but it was still better than adult prison. Anything was better than that.

"I accept the plea deal as set forth by your lawyers," said the judge, "and as such, the lesser crime of theft in the second degree, which is a class B misdemeanor."

Emily waited with bated breath, and when she heard "probation" and "community service," she wanted to burst into relieved tears. By the time the hearing was over, she was hugging Josh until he complained about not being able to breathe.

"Thank you," she said as she shook Harry's hand.

"He's the one who did all the work." Harry pointed to Phin with a wry smile.

Phin had noticeably stayed back, letting Emily hug her brother and thank the JCC officer. She wanted to launch herself into his arms, tell him that she loved him again. God, she loved him! At this moment, she didn't think she could love anyone more than she loved Phin Younger.

"So I get to go home and stay home?" Josh said.

Harry slapped him on the arm. "Yep, as long as you behave yourself. But I'll still be hounding you and meeting with you during your probation."

Josh sat down heavily in the chair he'd just occupied, his face in his hands. His shoulders shook, and Emily wrapped her arms around him. She didn't even notice when Phin and Harry left them alone.

"It's over, Joshie," she said tenderly, brushing his hair from his forehead. "It's over. It's over, and we can go home."

Josh kept shaking. "I didn't know if it would work. I thought the judge might throw out the deal, send me straight to prison—" He broke off, his voice cracking, and Emily realized in that moment that despite her brother's bravado, he was just a terrified kid in over his head.

"But he didn't. He saw that you were a decent kid, and he gave you a second chance. So don't waste it."

Josh shook his head. "I won't. I promise." He took a deep

breath. "I'm going to pay you back for everything. Even if it takes me a hundred years."

"You don't have to. You're my brother."

"Doesn't matter. I need to get my shit together." By the set of his shoulders, Emily could tell that her brother meant what he said.

She hated the shadows in his eyes from everything that had happened. She hated that the boy was gone, but she could appreciate the man he would become. She said a little prayer to any deity listening that he stayed on the right course.

"You should've let me rot," he said, shooting her a dark look. "I would have."

"No, you wouldn't have. You're my only family left, and my little brother. I would've gone to the ends of the earth for you."

That just made Josh shake his head and cover his face again, and Emily let him cry a little longer, murmuring into his ear until he calmed down.

They left the courthouse together. To Emily's surprise, Phin waited for them, sitting on a bench nearby. Her heart lifted into her throat as she looked at him.

"I need to talk to Phin. Wait for me?"

Josh's eyes narrowed. He stared over at Phin, as if he saw him in a completely new light. "What's between you guys?"

"Nothing," she stuttered. "Why do you think that?"

"Because he looks at you like you're the best thing he's ever seen." Josh's voice turned sly. "And you're red now. Are you macking on my lawyer, sis?"

Emily just turned a brighter red, and when Josh laughed, she almost couldn't get mad at him. It was the first true laugh she'd heard from him for so long.

"I know what you're going to say," said Emily quietly.

"What?"

"That he's not my type. That he's a lawyer, and I'm…"

"Has he said that to you?" Now Josh sounded pissed.

Emily's eyes widened at the fierceness in her brother's tone. "What? No, of course not. He's been nothing but a gentleman." She thought of how they'd had sex on his office desk and amended that statement. *Mostly a gentleman.* "He's not like any guy I've dated."

Josh snorted. "Good. Your exes were all assholes, Em. Especially Landon. I hated him. I wanted to punch him in his nose so many times."

"I would agree with that."

"Look, thinking about my sister and my lawyer makes me want to puke because you're my *sister*, but if he does anything to hurt you, I'll kill him."

At first Emily wanted to laugh, but seeing the seriousness in Josh's face, she knew he meant it. He'd suddenly become a man, willing to protect those he loved. Squeezing his arm, she said, "No murder, please. I'm not paying for those court bills."

She kissed Josh on the cheek, which earned her an embarrassed groan. As Emily watched her brother catch the bus to head home, she wasn't worried when she let him out of her sight. She hoped this trust between them could grow again. She'd missed her brother during all of this.

"Everything okay?" said Phin as he approached Emily.

"We talked. I think we'll be okay." She swallowed against the lump in her throat as she gazed up at Phin. His hair shone like a beacon in the autumn sun. "You didn't have to wait for me."

"But I always will," was his gruff reply.

They walked to Phin's car, but he made no move to get inside. As she leaned against the car door, she suddenly felt the weight of everything that had happened slam into her. The hearing, the sentencing, almost losing her brother forever.

She caught Phin's arm to steady her, her breathing harsh, and he wrapped her in his arms without a word. She buried her face in his shirt. He was so warm and solid and comforting. She clung to him like he was the one bit of flotsam being hurled down the current. He held her up, kept her safe, made her feel loved despite never saying the words.

"I've never met anyone like you. You amaze me."

"Me?" Emily was incredulous. "With all the people you've helped and worked with? That can't be true."

"It is true, because you're one of the few people I've ever met who doesn't expect anything in return." He caressed her cheek, marveling at her. "You make me want to be a better man."

She wasn't certain Phin could be better than he already was, but then he kissed her. All thoughts fled her mind under the onslaught of his kiss. He kissed her like he wanted to touch her very soul. Emily felt lightheaded, like she could float away if she didn't hold on to Phin.

She didn't know how long the kiss lasted. It could've been seconds or days. But when they parted, Phin's expression had turned stony. Her heart fell before she realized he wasn't looking at her. He was looking at something over her shoulder.

She turned to see a man that seemed familiar but, in her currently foggy state of mind, didn't compute as anyone she could care about. Phin, though, just gripped her harder.

The man grinned like he'd just won the lottery. "Don't mind me," he said with a laugh. "I didn't mean to interrupt."

The man kept walking, laughing to himself. A curl of fear snaked inside Emily. What had that all been about?

"Who was that?" she said.

Phin scowled. "Nobody you need to worry about."

"Based on how hard you're frowning, I should worry. Don't keep this from me. I can handle it."

Phin's jaw clenched, and Emily wondered if he'd tell her. But then he sighed and put space between them. Emily felt bereft when his hands moved away from her waist.

"That was Sterling McIntosh. He works for the district attorney. We have a…history."

Emily glanced over her shoulder, but Sterling had already driven away. "He seemed pretty happy to see you."

"He was happy because he saw that I was kissing you."

"What? I don't understand."

"I didn't want to tell you because I didn't want you to take this as your burden." When she would've protested, he added, "I know you. You would've blamed yourself. Sterling has been out to screw me over for years, and he's been sniffing around extra close because of our relationship."

"Does he think you took advantage of me?"

"Oh, that's what he'll say." Phin put his hands into his pockets.

"Could this hurt your job? Oh God, could you get fired? Or worse?" Panic clawed at Emily's throat. She hadn't even thought about how this would affect Phin. How could she be so selfish.

"Stop. I know what you're thinking. It was my decision to make, and I've meant to have a reckoning with Sterling for a long time now. He doesn't scare me."

Phin drew her into his arms, but Emily couldn't believe a

word he said. She didn't understand all the details. But she knew that powerful men with an axe to grind and money to spend were the most powerful enemies you could have. And if this Sterling wanted to make Phin's life hell because of her? That thought sent her mind into a tailspin.

"I forbid you to worry about this," said Phin when he dropped her off at her apartment thirty minutes later. His tone brooked no argument. "It's not your fight. It's mine."

"But it's my fault you're fighting at all."

"It would've happened sooner or later. Don't blame yourself. Okay?" He kissed her forehead.

Even though she nodded, agreeing to his demands, inside she knew she had to do something. She couldn't sit on the sidelines as Phin fought for the most important thing in his life —his career.

Because if she were the one to destroy that? She'd never forgive herself.

CHAPTER TWENTY-ONE

It took Phin a week to admit to Emily that Sterling had submitted an official complaint to the bar association. It was late at night. Emily curled up next to Phin, but neither of them could sleep.

She had known something was eating at him. He kept telling her it was nothing, but with enough badgering, he'd caved and told her the news.

Now, they both lay silently. Emily's mind whirled with how she could fix this for Phin. She knew he would tell her to leave well enough alone, and it wasn't that she didn't trust that he knew what he was talking about. It was more that she knew that she'd caused this to happen in the first place.

"I'll take care of it," said Phin into the dark room. "I didn't want to tell you because I knew you'd worry."

Emily didn't answer. She didn't know whether to find it comforting that he didn't want to worry her, or to be annoyed that he thought she was so fragile that she couldn't handle the truth.

A few days later, she sat in the district attorney's office, waiting for her appointment. She kept tapping her foot against the pale green carpet, her nerves shot. She went over in her mind what she'd decided to say. At this point, it was like lines from a play repeating in her brain. She could probably say everything in her sleep.

"Mr. McIntosh will see you now."

Emily followed a woman to a nondescript office. When the door closed behind Emily and she faced the man who wanted to hurt Phin so badly, she couldn't help but think that he seemed rather small, sitting in his chair.

He motioned for her to come forward without looking up. "Sit down, Ms. Lassiter. I'll be with you in a moment."

His politeness threatened to throw Emily off-balance. Already on edge, she didn't know how to take him. Then again, maybe he wanted to put her off-balance. Weren't lawyers good at things like that?

She sat on the edge of the chair, purse clutched in her lap, trying not to look around the office but not failing to notice that Sterling had far fewer books in his office than Phin did. He did, however, have his degrees hung in prominent spots, the glass faces shining in the fluorescent lighting. Someone must dust them on a weekly basis, she thought.

"I have to say, I was surprised when I saw your name on my calendar. I almost thought my assistant was playing a joke on me." Sterling smiled, all congeniality. "But here you are, in the flesh."

When Emily had done her first runway show, she'd been so nervous that she'd almost vomited. One of the older models had taken her under her wing and had told her that if she focused on a spot on the wall in front of her and didn't look at the audience, she wouldn't get overwhelmed.

But Sterling wasn't an audience of hundreds, and she couldn't act like she found him intimidating. She held his gaze without wavering, even when his smile widened until his teeth flashed.

"I wanted to talk to you about Phin Younger," she said.

"I figured as much, although I should warn you, you're wasting your time."

She ignored that comment. "He wouldn't tell me the history between you two, but Mr. Younger has been nothing but a help to me and my brother, Josh. Without him, Josh most likely would've been charged with something far more serious and faced prison time. Mr. Younger is a credit to his profession. I can't speak highly enough of him—"

Sterling help up a hand. "Spare me the letter of recommendation. Why should I believe you? Or rather, believe that you're unbiased when I saw with my own eyes what he was doing?"

"Relationships with clients aren't illegal."

"No, but that doesn't mean they're ethical, either. And you coming here just shows that I was right to submit a complaint." Sterling's smile turned into a sneer. "Did he send you here on his behalf?"

"Of course not. He doesn't know I'm here."

Sterling barked a laugh. "God, it gets even better. His avenging angel. Or should I say pleading angel? Did you think you could come on bended knee and get me to change my mind?" His expression turned into one that made Emily's blood turn cold. "How far are you willing to plead for your boyfriend, Ms. Lassiter? Now I'm curious."

She trembled, but she refused to show that she was now

afraid. "I'm willing to submit any kind of evidence that your complaint isn't true."

"Then why come to me?" He rounded his desk until he stood over her. Although he was hardly a man of stature, there was a malice to Sterling that only a fool couldn't see. "I think you're willing to go a lot further than you'd admit out loud. You know, it's funny—I looked you up when I found out Phin was sniffing around you. And surprise, surprise, that I find you've done some very racy modeling photos in the past few months. Does Phin know that his girlfriend is getting paid to show her tits to other men? I'd love to know."

Emily couldn't breathe at the venom in Sterling's words. When his finger traced a line on her hand, she froze, like a rabbit caught in the jaws of a wolf. For a moment, she saw this happening from a distance. She wondered why she couldn't move, couldn't speak, couldn't react.

"I can see why Phin put his career in jeopardy, though, no matter your past. You're beautiful. Way too beautiful for the likes of him. What do you see in him? He's hardly rich, and he's a total prig. You'd think a woman like you would have better taste."

"You mean I should be interested in you instead?" Emily tried to make the words harsh, but she was shaking too much for the insult to land.

"You're not stupid." Sterling smiled. "So, let's make a deal. Give me what I want, and you can save your precious Mr. Younger. Let me show you what a real man can do for you."

Emily took a deep breath. She thought of Phin. She thought of how brave he was. She thought of everything between them, all the words said and the ones unsaid. And then in a burst of adrenaline, she pushed Sterling so hard that he tipped backward and caught his hip on the edge of his desk. He crashed to the floor in a heap of limbs, swearing colorfully.

"I came here because Phin deserves someone to defend him. I don't care what you say to me, but he's twice the man you are. No matter what you try to do to him, he will never stoop to your level."

Sterling stood up, his eyes blazing. "If you think I'll lift a finger to help him now—"

"Of course you won't. I should've known better, but I thought maybe you'd have something inside you that was good and just." Her lips twisted. "I assumed you might have some shred of decency. That might make me naive, but at least I haven't turned into a malicious little man like you."

Sterling just stared at her, like he didn't know what she was. She could almost pity him—almost. If he hadn't come after the man she loved, she could've felt some bit of pity for him.

"You've opened Pandora's box," sneered Sterling as he returned to his side of the desk. "This isn't over."

Emily smiled. "Go fuck yourself, Sterling," was her bright sally before she waved goodbye.

AT THE END of the week, Linda finally called Phin into her office with a drawn expression on her face. "You seem rather calm about all of this," she remarked.

"I've done nothing wrong, so, yes, I'm calm."

Linda hesitated, her lips parted. She drummed her fingers on her desk. "I actually have an interesting bit of news."

"Even more interesting than Sterling submitting a complaint about me?"

"Believe it or not, yes."

Phin blinked in surprise. What else could Sterling throw onto the burning pile that was this mess? It wasn't as if Phin had some other deep dark secret for Sterling to unearth. Then again, there was no telling what Sterling might try next.

"I had an interesting phone call from Janice. You know Janice, from the DA's office? Anyway, she told me that Sterling had a meeting with none other than Ms. Lassiter herself."

Phin let out a startled laugh, but based on Linda's expression, she wasn't joking. "You can't be serious."

"Janice is a lot of things, but she's honest. Besides, why make up something like that? Janice being Janice, she told me about the meeting."

"I never once told Emily to do such a thing. I can't believe she would go to Sterling. Of all people!" Phin rose from his chair and began to pace, because sitting seemed so casual right then. He could barely wrap his head around Linda's words. Why had Emily done such a thing?

For a millisecond, he wondered if Emily was in cahoots with Sterling, but he dismissed the idea. He trusted her implicitly. But why do it?

"I can't tell you what happened or what they talked about, but Janice saw Sterling burst from his office not twenty minutes later, looking like he wanted to burn something down." Linda smiled widely. "So I'm going to guess it went well."

"I have to talk to Emily. What if Sterling did something to her?" He remembered finding Sterling and Melissa, how terrified Melissa had been. He'd never forget it. The thought that

Sterling had touched Emily made him want to draw blood. He'd break Sterling's neck himself if he so much as looked at Emily the wrong way.

"I don't think even Sterling would try something in the DA's office. Sit down, Phin. Your pacing is giving me a headache."

He sat, albeit unwillingly. "Why tell me this?"

"Before Janice called me, I was going to give you completely different advice with all of this. I wanted you to say that Ms. Lassiter pursued you. Make it sound like she threw herself at you, and that you would have nothing to do with her going forward."

Phin stilled, staring at his boss. Her cold-blooded suggestion to throw Emily under the proverbial bus made his own blood boil—even if she'd supposedly changed her mind. Logically, he understood what she was saying. He probably would've given her the same advice, under the circumstances. But that was before he'd met Emily.

"I would never do that," he said without hesitation.

"I figured as much. And the fact that she went into the enemy's lair says a lot. She was willing to take that risk for you." Linda smiled before saying wryly, "I'm hardly a romantic, but even I can see that she must care a whole hell of a lot about you to do that."

Phin felt like his heart might disintegrate at those words. Emily had told him that she loved him, and he'd said nothing. He'd thought for so long that love wasn't for him. But Emily had already proven that he was wrong. So wrong.

He'd been right about one thing: he didn't deserve her. Yet if he could spend the rest of his life working to deserve her, he'd consider it a life well spent.

"She told me she loved me."

"Well, there you go."

Phin put his head in his hands. "I didn't say it back. God, I'm a fucking idiot."

"You still have time. I mean, I'm perpetually single and incapable of dating, but I can tell you that she's probably waiting for you right now to tell her that."

"When did you become the love doctor?"

"Since you turned my office into a soap opera."

Phin laughed, then said seriously. "I won't desert Emily, no matter how logical your suggestion is. She's everything to me."

"If you said otherwise, you wouldn't be the man I've always known and respected." She rose and put out her hand. "I wish you luck. I hope this all comes to nothing. I truly do."

Phin shook her hand. "I appreciate your support, regardless."

"Do you think there are people lining up to be public defenders? I might be sentimental today, but I'm not stupid. Now, go get your lady already, and if you tell anyone we had this conversation, I'll have you committed."

CHAPTER TWENTY-TWO

Strangely enough, Emily felt almost energized after her encounter with Sterling. Or maybe it was just the left-over adrenaline that kept her smiling and laughing and taking orders that evening, like she didn't have a care in the world.

If she thought too hard about what Sterling had said, she knew she would stop smiling. And if she thought about how Phin would react once he found out? Well, she decided that she'd think about that later. Preferably in a million years, when it might not seem so daunting.

On her break, she wandered into the kitchen and sat down heavily on a stool in the corner. Her stomach rumbled with hunger, but she ignored it. She was still too on edge to keep anything down.

Jenson eyed her as he finished slapping a hamburger together. "You look like shit," he said without preamble.

"You're such a charmer."

He grunted. "Just speaking the truth." His eyes narrowed as he took in her appearance. Emily had thought she looked as she always did, but then again, Jenson was surprisingly perceptive for a line cook. "What happened?"

"Nothing I can explain in the ten minutes I have left of my break."

Another waitress burst into the kitchen, and after Jenson told her to hold her horses, she took her order with an annoyed sniff. Lawrence had just hired that one—Emily couldn't remember her name. Joanna? Jane? Something with a J. She'd probably last a week, tops.

"Now you have five minutes," said Jenson.

Emily sighed, tugging on her braid. That adrenaline? It was gone now, to be replaced with a cold pit of fear. "I did something that I thought would help somebody, but I think I just made things worse."

Jenson waited.

"I wanted to make things right because what happened was partially my fault. Now I'm afraid that the person I helped will hate me."

Jenson turned to flip some sizzling burgers. Emily glanced at the cracked clock on the wall, knowing that she needed to return to work in only a few minutes. Lawrence was a good boss, but he hated when anyone took more than fifteen minutes for their break.

Jenson began slapping burgers together with the speed of a man who'd made thousands of them before. "When I met Claudia, I couldn't get work. Not after I'd gotten out of the Army. She called in a favor with some guy she knew. I got the job, not knowing she'd done that. When I found out, I was pissed."

Emily wasn't sure what this had to do with her situation, but it was also the most Jenson had ever spoken to her.

"When I told Claudia that I didn't accept handouts or charity, she told me that the strongest people were always the dumbest because they thought asking for help was weak."

"So I guess you stayed at the job?" said Emily.

Jenson set a completed plate under the heater. "No, but I figured out that anybody who thinks somebody helping them is a bad thing isn't a person worth being around."

"You're saying if the guy I helped takes it badly…"

Jenson shrugged. "Ain't sayin' nothing. Now get back to work before Lawrence notices you in here."

Emily worked the rest of the afternoon as if in a daze, considering Jenson's words. He was right, in a way. But she also knew that the effect of one's actions mattered as much as —and oftentimes more than—the intentions behind them.

Her only wish right then was to get off work and to find Phin. She'd considered calling him after she'd left Sterling's office, but that had seemed so impersonal. She needed to confess everything in person. She owed him that, at the very least.

She'd just taken a family of four's orders when the front doorbell jangled. When Emily looked up from her notepad, she almost dropped it into the lap of the seven-year-old in astonishment.

It was Phin. Here, at her work. She couldn't breathe.

"Ma'am, are you okay?" the mother asked.

"I'm fine," squeaked Emily as Phin approached her.

She searched his expression. She couldn't tell if he was angry with her or not. But why would he be? He didn't know what she'd done. He didn't seem happy, though. He had that poker-face-lawyer expression that she both admired and hated.

"What are you doing here?" she said.

He looked so handsome that her heart almost burst. He wore his usual suit and tie, sans jacket, his hair rumpled. He shot her a faint smile.

"Can we talk?"

Emily heard footsteps that sounded like Lawrence's. "I just took my break. I'm not off for another three hours. I'm sorry."

Phin glanced at the family staring up at them. The younger child, who couldn't have been more than four years old, popped her thumb into her mouth and watched the entire tableau with avid interest.

"Then I'll say what I have to say right here." His eyes flashed. "I know what you did—that you talked to Sterling on my behalf."

Emily rather wished the ground would open up and swallow her right then and there. Could you die of humiliation? She was so startled that Phin already knew what she'd done that it was like she had no more words to speak.

"Linda, my boss, told me today. When she told me, at first I thought it was a joke. Part of me still doesn't believe it."

"It happened," whispered Emily.

Phin's jaw clenched. "Why? Why would you do that?" He seemed anguished as he asked the question, and Emily's heart sank into her toes.

"Emily, is this guy bothering you?" said Lawrence. He approached Phin, his arms crossed. "I don't let people harass my employees. Either get a table or get out."

"He's not bothering me. He's a…" Emily scrambled for the right descriptor. *Lover? Boyfriend? Man I love but who might hate me now because I'm an idiot?*

"A friend," she said weakly.

Phin flinched.

Lawrence's eyes were narrowed. "Then I'd recommend you get a table and order something," was all he said before returning to the back.

Emily almost burst into hysterical giggles.

"Which section is yours?" Phin asked, all seriousness.

"Um, this is mine. You can have that table by the dividing wall."

Phin sat at the table specified without protest. To Emily's frustration, she had to tend to her other tables first. She could feel Lawrence watching her like a hawk. She knew it wasn't because he didn't trust her—he just didn't trust Phin. Besides, the diner was so busy right then that Emily couldn't take another break anytime soon.

By the time she went to Phin's table and asked what he wanted to order, Phin looked fit to be tied.

"You can't take a five-minute break?" he hissed. "Seriously?"

"Rules are rules." And for some reason, she wanted to see how badly he wanted to talk to her. If he wanted to chew her out, he could do it while ordering a plate of food and tipping her for the service.

"This is absurd." He sighed, rumpling his hair further. "Why did you go to Sterling, Emily? Why would you do such a thing?"

She stared at him, as if the answer were obvious. To her, it *was* obvious. Hadn't she already told him?

"Because I love you," she said simply, any amusement wiped from her tone. "And I was the one who got you into trouble. I wanted to make it right."

A stark expression crossed Phin's face. "Why?"

"Why what?"

"Why would you love me?"

In that moment, the entire diner melted away. It was if they were the only two people in existence. Hearing his words, the hoarseness of his voice, made her want to kiss him until he understood how much she loved him.

"If you were anyone else, I'd think you were fishing for compliments. But not you. Why do you think I love you?" she said quietly.

"I don't know."

"You're kind. Honorable. Thoughtful. Smart. Handsome, of course." She crouched down so they were at eye level. "And I just love you. That's all. Sometimes things just are because they are."

He let out a gruff laugh. "That makes no sense."

"Look, I'm sure you're angry about what I did—"

"Angry? Yes, I'm angry." He looked away a long moment. "I'm angry because you put yourself in the line of fire for me. You could've been hurt. You don't know what Sterling is capable of. You went to him by yourself, not caring about your own safety, because of *me*." His voice broke. "I don't deserve something like that."

"It's not a matter of deserving. I did it because I love you. Even if you never love me back—"

"Never love you? Christ, Emily, I'm about to fall apart because I love you so much." He pulled her into a tight hug that threatened to cut off her breathing. "I love you so much I can't bear it. The thought of you in Sterling's office is like torture."

Emily clutched at Phin, tears springing to her eyes, realizing that he loved her. It was a miracle. It was too much.

Phin tipped her head up so he could gaze into her eyes. "I love you, Emily. I should've told you ages ago, but I'm a coward. Can you forgive me?"

"There's nothing to forgive."

He groaned before kissing her with such passion that she was glad she wasn't standing, because she would've fallen to her knees. It was only through the haze of joy and desire that she heard someone clear their throat over her shoulder.

"This has been a great show," said Lawrence wryly, "but how about you take it to my office before it turns R rated?"

Emily looked up and realized that the entire diner was staring at them both. The mother of the family was crying; another customer dabbed at his eyes with a napkin, sniffling loudly.

Phin rose and then swooped down to pick up Emily in his arms. "Sorry for interrupting your meals," he called, his eyes sparkling, "but the next part of the show is for our eyes only."

Emily blushed scarlet at the implication. Laughter trailed after them as they went to Lawrence's office. By the time Phin had shut the door and set her down, he was kissing her again. She moaned his name, pushing against him, like she wanted to crawl under his skin. She couldn't get enough of him.

Phin kissed down her throat. "If you ever do something as crazy as go to Sterling again," he said in warning tones, "I'll take you over my knee."

"That doesn't sound as terrible as you'd think."

Growling, he bit down onto her shoulder—not enough to hurt, but enough to leave a mark. His hands were everywhere

—cupping her breasts, palming her ass, sliding up her shirt to the bare skin of her back.

Emily tried to unbutton Phin's shirt, but impatient, she decided she'd rather just rip it open. Buttons flew every which way.

"We shouldn't do this in your boss's office," said Phin, even as he unzipped her jeans and cupped her mound.

"Then we better be so quiet that he never suspects."

Emily tried her best to keep quiet, but it was difficult when Phin pressed a finger inside her while rubbing her clit with the heel of his hand. He had to cover her mouth as she came with just a few strokes.

But then it was his turn to lose his mind. Emily pushed him down into a chair and took his cock into her mouth. Licking him from root to tip, she inhaled his masculine scent, loving the way he gripped her hair each time she moved her mouth down his cock.

"I want to come inside your pussy," whispered Phin. Emily shivered, her sex clenching at his dirty words.

Soon, she sat on his lap and sank down onto him. The chair creaked under their weight. She rode him slowly at first, his cock stretching her almost to the point of it being too much, until the only sensation she could feel was sheer pleasure. She picked up the pace as Phin dug his fingers into her hips.

A low groan sounded in Phin's throat. When he started to come, Emily kissed him to cover the sound. The feeling of his cock twitching inside her triggered her own orgasm. He filled her with washes of heat, and she clenched around him for so long she wondered if this was her longest orgasm ever.

They were a rumpled, sweaty heap of limbs afterward. Emily couldn't move, even if she wanted to.

"I need to get back to work," she said halfheartedly.

Phin gripped her tightly. "No way in hell."

She laughed softly. "We can't both get fired from our jobs, you know."

At that, Phin's expression turned serious. "My boss recommended that I deny our relationship to the bar association."

Emily couldn't breathe.

"But I told her that my career is nothing if you're not at my side." He brushed a few strands of hair from her forehead. "You're more important than my career. And I'd never throw you under the bus to save myself."

"I don't want you to sacrifice yourself for me like that." She swallowed hard. "Maybe your boss is right. Even if you deny our relationship, that doesn't mean we couldn't date later on."

"And tell the world that you don't matter? That I don't love you?" He made her look him in the eye. "You are everything. *Everything.* I'm never letting you go—no matter what."

Realizing that he spoke the absolute truth, Emily's heart thrilled. Bursting with love, all she could do was kiss him and show him that she felt exactly the same way.

EPILOGUE

Emily closed her eyes as she lay down on the soft grass. With the sun shining and the breeze cool, it was the first truly warm day of spring. After a little persuasion, she'd managed to get Phin to agree to picnic at Willamette Park, not far from Emily's apartment.

It wasn't that Phin didn't want to spend time with her. On the contrary, they spent as much time together as either could manage. It was just that Phin enjoyed spending *private* time with Emily, and he told her with a heated smile that he couldn't seduce her when little kids and old people were within close proximity.

"What are you smiling about?" said Phin as he sat down next to her.

She opened one eye. "Do I have to have a specific reason?"

"I thought this morning might be the reason why you're smiling."

Considering what they'd done this morning—and where—Emily just smiled wider and closed her eyes again.

Phin didn't say anything for a while, but Emily knew it wasn't because he was keeping something from her. They often had moments like this, where neither spoke but simply basked in each other's company. Emily would oftentimes find Phin deep in thought, and she'd sit next to him until he decided to talk. Emily had never been much for sitting and simply thinking, but she could enjoy watching Phin's bouts of contemplation.

Phin also no longer had the heavy burden of Sterling's complaint hanging over his head. With Emily's own testimony, coupled with a lack of evidence that Phin had actually jeopardized Josh Lassiter's case or had taken advantage of Emily, the complaint had been dismissed. Although Emily had known from the beginning that Phin would be exonerated, he hadn't been as confident.

Perhaps that made her naive. She preferred to consider herself optimistic. With Phin in her life now, it was easy to be optimistic.

She also had told Phin about the nude photos she'd done when she'd been desperate. He hadn't been happy about them, only because he'd hated that she'd done something she hadn't wanted to do just to survive. "Take whatever photos you want and make all the money you want," he'd said, "but keep the nude ones just for me, okay?"

That hadn't been a difficult bargain to fulfill, to say the least.

"Emily," said Phin softly. He brushed her forehead with gentle fingers. "Are you awake?"

She giggled. "With you touching me, yes." She sat up with a yawn and stretched luxuriously, Phin's gaze heating as her breasts rose and fell. "Like what you see?"

"Always." He kissed her, long and leisurely, and Emily almost wished they weren't in a public park. Then again, there were woods around here. Maybe they could sneak away and find a private nook…

"Jesus, get a room."

Emily shot her younger brother an impish grin. "We already have one that we use regularly."

Josh's cheeks turned red. "*Emily*…"

"Don't terrorize your brother." Phin motioned for Josh to sit. "Emily didn't tell me that she invited guests to our picnic."

"I like to keep you on your toes," she replied.

Josh, who had already grown taller since the fall, now sported a dark beard and had let his hair grow out. Emily didn't like it, only because he seemed so much older.

It had been a struggle for Josh to get back on track in terms of school, but Emily was immensely proud of his determination to graduate on time. He was entering senior year with all of the credits necessary despite the weeks missed after his arrest.

Emily knew that a huge reason for Josh staying on the right path had been Phin's influence. His quiet but mature presence in Josh's life had provided the father figure that Josh had needed for so long. Josh hadn't been a fan of Phin dating Emily at first. But Phin had worked his magic on the teenager without Phin even realizing he was doing it. Emily liked to call it the Phin Effect.

"You make people want to be better," she'd told him one night.

Phin had stared at her. "Me? How?"

"The fact that you don't know the answer is why."

Phin had frowned at her, demanded to know what she

meant, and had eventually decided that in lieu of a real answer, he'd seduce her a second time that night.

"What classes are you planning on taking in the fall?" said Phin to Josh.

"Physics, Lit, and European History." Josh was studiously not looking at either Emily or Phin as he said quietly, "I wanted to take this one other class that they started offering, but it was full."

"Which one? Spanish?" said Emily.

"No. It's an intro to law studies." Josh glanced up at Phin, then looked away again.

"Do you want to go to law school?" said Emily, hope rising inside her.

Josh shrugged. "I dunno if I can. But it sounds cool. Thought I might as well take some intro class on it."

Emily waited for Phin to say something, but he was silent right then. This was one instance where she wished he wouldn't be silent. Couldn't he see that Josh was on pins and needles waiting for Phin to say something?

"I've always heard that lots of English majors end up in law school. You'll definitely want to focus on writing if you decide that's what you want to do," said Emily.

"Like I said, I don't know if I even want to do it. It just sounds better than other shit people want to do."

Emily poked Phin in the side, but he ignored her.

Finally, Phin spoke. "If you end up deciding that you want to apply to law schools, let me know. I can write you a recommendation letter and introduce you to the right people."

"Like it'll really happen." Now Josh sounded irritated.

Before Emily could console her younger brother, Phin said, "Who's to say it won't? If you want it, do it. You're smart enough, and you've shown that when you try, you can accomplish a lot. That's more than most people can say, believe me."

Josh looked like Phin had just given him the elixir of life, although he'd never admit it. Instead he just shrugged, got up, and said, "I'll see you later. Don't get arrested for indecent exposure."

"That kid," muttered Emily. "He's going to be the death of me."

"But soon he'll be off your hands. He's almost an adult."

She sighed. "I know. That's the worst thing of all."

Phin pressed a kiss to her temple. She hugged him, feeling his heart beat under her palm, loving him all the more that he loved her brother, thorns and all.

"Thank you for what you said to him. He needs all the encouragement he can get."

"I told him the truth. He can do it if he really wants it."

"I'm just glad he's not dyslexic like me. He's smart enough to do whatever he wants in life."

Phin tilted her head back so he could look into her eyes. "Emily, you're the smartest woman I've ever met. No, I'm not being nice to you. Do you think I call stupid people smart on a daily basis?"

She gurgled a laugh. "Of course not."

"Then believe me. I've also been meaning to tell you that if you want me to help you study for your GED, I will. Or pay for classes. Whatever you want. I know you can get it because God knows you're even more determined than your brother."

Her old insecurities threatened to resurface, but Phin's confidence in her bolstered her own. "I want to finally get my GED, then. No more excuses. I'm ready."

At that, Phin reached into the picnic basket and pulled out

her GED textbooks, which she'd ignored since the fall. She gaped at him.

"How did you—did you plan this?"

"Not to the degree you're thinking. I just thought I'd bring up the subject again. Your brother was an extra to the conversation."

She shook her head, marveling at him. Then she snagged the book from him, grabbed a pen from her purse, and said, "Then let's get started, Professor. Teach me everything you know."

"I'd love nothing more." Then he kissed her under the spring sunshine.

Lucy Younger had fallen in love with acting when she was in kindergarten. She'd been in the school play and had played a squirrel trying to steal a nut from a tree. When she'd improvised half her lines, her teacher had scolded her later, but she'd known that the laughs she'd gotten from the crowd were something she'd never forget.

Now, though, she wondered if her kindergarten self would forgive her for taking the part of Crazed Menstruating Woman. It was a commercial for some PMS medication, and Lucy had snagged the part of a woman who couldn't stop haranguing her poor husband, crying, and eating cheese puffs because she hadn't had the foresight to pick up the medication at the local drugstore.

"Cut! Lucy, can you really sob this time? Not just a few tears like you've watched a sad movie. I mean, crying because your boyfriend dumped you and your dog died all in the same day," said the director.

Lucy thought of how she wanted to be a serious actress and had failed at that goal during the almost ten years she'd lived in Los Angeles. She thought of how she was doing this commercial. Both were enough to get her to really sob in earnest.

By the time she returned to her dump of an apartment, Lucy stared at the stack of bills on the countertop and considered giving up. She was barely paying her exorbitant rent. The few commercials she'd booked weren't enough to live in Los Angeles. She worked as a barista, but even that wasn't enough. It didn't help that her roommate had bounced to live with her boyfriend, and Lucy hadn't yet found someone to replace her.

Or maybe she just wanted to wallow by herself for once.

She had twenty dollars in the bank, no savings, and nothing but bills and credit card debt to her name. As she shuffled through her bills, she winced when she saw the multiple envelopes stamped with OVERDUE. She decided to bury those envelopes underneath the stack.

If she didn't look at them, then they didn't exist—right?

But Lucy couldn't return home with her tail between her legs. Her brothers had hated that she'd left Fair Haven, Washington, and they'd told her that she'd struggle to achieve her dream. It wasn't that they didn't believe in her; they just worried. Thea, her older sister, was also an artist (a graphic novelist, to be exact), so she'd been more supportive over the years.

If she gave this all up and went back, her brothers would tell her they'd been right. And that thought alone was unbearable. She wouldn't give up yet. Not when her next big break could be right around the corner. As they always said in Hollywood, you never know when opportunity will come knocking.

Well, nobody said that, exactly, but Lucy did. Lucy had to say it to herself.

Lucy was eating her nightly bowl of ramen noodles with an egg on top for some cheap protein when her agent called her.

"I have a gig for you," said Wendy in excited tones. "In a movie, Lucy. Not a commercial, not some random play. A movie!"

Lucy almost dropped her bowl of noodles onto her feet. Her hands trembling, she set the bowl down on the coffee table instead. "Are you serious?"

"So fucking serious. So serious that I called you on a Saturday night when I should be getting banged out by some hottie I picked up at The Pink Clam."

Lucy snorted. "If you feel a burning sensation later on, it's definitely chlamydia."

"Fuck off," said Wendy cheerily. "No, listen to me. This is for a lead role in an indie flick. The audition is on Tuesday, in the Valley. Get it, and you'll be filming on Hazel Island for the entire summer."

"That's not far from my hometown."

"Fascinating. I already put you down for the audition. I know you can get it. You're perfect for this part. I emailed you the script and everything. Don't let me down."

Lucy's ramen noodles were forgotten as she read through the script and the character description. Her heart pounded faster and faster with excitement as she read each word.

When she saw the director and producers attached, she

knew that this movie could be the role of a lifetime. She wanted it so badly she could taste it.

I'm going to get this part, she vowed, *and I'm going to spend the summer on Hazel.*

If she got the part, it'd be more than enough money to support her for the next six months, and she wouldn't have to go home with her tail between her legs.

Taking a deep breath, she pressed *print* on the script and got to work.

ABOUT THE AUTHOR

A coffee addict and cat lover, Iris Morland writes sexy and funny contemporary romances. If she's not reading or writing, she enjoys binging on Netflix shows and cooking something delicious.